About the Author

Nathan Dylan Goodwin was born and raised in Hastings, East Sussex. Schooled in the town, he then completed a Bachelor of Arts degree in Radio, Film and Television, followed by a Master of Arts Degree in Creative Writing at Canterbury Christ Church University. A member of the Society of Authors, he has completed a number of successful local history books about Hastings, as well as other works of fiction in this series; other interests include reading, photography, running, skiing, travelling and of course, genealogy. He is a member of the Guild of One-Name Studies and the Society of Genealogists, as well as being a member of the Sussex Family History Group, the Norfolk Family History Society, the Kent Family History Society and the Hastings and Rother Family History Society. He lives in Kent with his partner and son.

BY THE SAME AUTHOR

nonfiction:
Hastings at War 1939-1945 (2005)
Hastings Wartime Memories and Photographs (2008)
Hastings & St Leonards Through Time (2010)
Around Battle Through Time (2012)

fiction:
(The Forensic Genealogist series)
Hiding the Past (2013)
The Lost Ancestor (2014)
The Orange Lilies (2014) – *A Morton Farrier novella*
The America Ground (2015)
The Spyglass File (2016)
The Missing Man (2017) – *A Morton Farrier novella*

The Missing Man
by
Nathan Dylan Goodwin

Copyright © Nathan Dylan Goodwin 2017

Nathan Dylan Goodwin has asserted his right under the Copyright, Designs and Patents Act 1998 to be identified as the author of this work.

This story is a work of fiction. Names and characters are the product of the author's imagination and any resemblance to actual persons, living or dead, is entirely coincidental. Where the names of real people have been used, they appear only as the author imagined them to be.

All rights reserved. No part of this publication may be reproduced, stored in a retrieval system, or transmitted by any means, without the prior permission in writing of the author. This story is sold subject to the condition that it shall not, by way of trade or otherwise, be lent, resold, hired out, or otherwise circulated without the author's prior consent in any form of binding, cover or other eformat, including this condition being imposed on the subsequent purchaser.

Cover design: Patrick Dengate
www.patrickdengate.com

For my dad, Dennis Leslie Goodwin
One of the good ones, taken too soon

Prologue

24th December 1976, Hyannis Port, Massachusetts, USA

Velda was numb. The blanket over her shoulders, now heavy from the falling snow, did nothing to stop the acute quivering that rattled through her body. The police tape barricade, vibrating in the icy wind against her hands, had confined her to the street. The swelling congregation behind her—a motley mixture of prying and anxious neighbours and the whole gamut of emergency service personnel—were rendered faceless by the darkness of the night.

Velda's eyes followed the thick snakes of white hose that crossed her lawn from the hydrant, into the hands of the firefighters, who were battling the great rasping flames that projected from every window of the house. *Her* house.

One of the firefighters—the chief, she assumed—approached her. He was sweating and his face was marked with black blotches. 'Ma'am—are you *sure* your husband and daughter are still inside?'

'Yes,' she heard herself say.

'They couldn't have slipped out to get something from the grocery store or...?'

'No,' Velda sobbed. 'They're inside. Please find them.'

The fire chief nodded and turned back towards the house.

A moment later, without fanfare or warning, the house collapsed. The shocked gasps of her neighbours and the stricken cries of the firefighters on the lawn were lost to the appalling cacophony of metal, brick, wood and glass crumbling together, crescendo-ing into the night sky. A funnel of dense black smoke, peppered with flecks of bright red and orange, clashed in mid-air with the flurrying of falling snow.

Then, an odd stillness.

That her house—her *home*—could be reduced to this pile of indescribable burning debris in front of her shocked her anew.

This wasn't how it was supposed to be.

The hermetic seal that had neatly separated past and present had just ruptured spectacularly.

And now it was all over.

Somebody touched her shoulder and said something. She turned. It was her son, Jack. Either Velda's ears were still ringing with the sound of the house disintegrating, or Jack was speaking soundlessly. There was an urgency to his voice.

Velda tried to reply but a sagging sensation in her heart emanated out under her skin and down into her quivering limbs. Her legs buckled from beneath her and she crumpled helplessly into the snow.

Chapter One

14th August 2016, Boston, Massachusetts, USA

Morton Farrier was shattered. He looked at his watch: just gone ten in the morning. He and his new wife, Juliette, had arrived at Logan International Airport late last night, following their marriage yesterday in their home town of Rye, England. He yawned. It was what—just after five in the morning in the UK?—and here he was sitting at a digital microfilm reader in Boston Public Library. He stretched and glanced around him. Having managed to navigate his way through busy and noisy corridors, courtyards and vast swathes of uninterrupted bookshelves, Morton now found himself in the genealogy section, tucked behind a partition at the rear of a palatial hall, where only fragmented whispers from the researchers working under green-shaded desk lamps reached the high ceiling above.

An almost tangible restlessness burrowed into Morton's insides, rendering him tense and apprehensive. He and Juliette were here on a three-week honeymoon, during which time he had the challenging task of locating his biological father. 'Come on, hurry up…' he muttered, looking behind him to the help desk where he had just requested a microfilm copy of the *Cape Cod Times* for December 1976. The year that was pivotal to his quest. The year that his paternal grandfather had died in a fire. The year that Morton's father had disappeared, aged twenty, from the face of the earth.

His notepad was open to a blank page, poised ready. Beneath it were the three letters that had spun his already complicated family tree onto a whole other level. His biological father, having no knowledge that his brief holiday romance in England in January 1974 had resulted in a child, had written to Morton's biological mother, telling her that he had discovered something from his own father's past. Something bad. Morton had found the three letters just as they had been when they had left the shores of Massachusetts in 1976; unopened and unread.

'Here you go.' Morton turned to see the young man from the help desk standing beside him. He placed a boxed microfilm down on the desk. 'Used one of these before?'

'Yes—a few times.'

'Okay, cool. Well, good luck—come find me if you need any further help.'

'Thank you.' He pulled the film from the box, threaded it through the machine, then buzzed on until the first edition of the newspaper appeared onscreen. He briefly took in the front page and established that the *Cape Cod Times* was published daily. He wound the film on until he reached the edition for the December 26th, 1976. And there it was, the headline story. *Devastating House Fire.* Below it was a large black and white photograph of a burning building. Morton zoomed into the story.

HYANNIS PORT-Holiday tragedy struck Velda Jacklin's family when a fire, apparently begun in a Christmas tree, killed her husband and injured her daughter. "She'll never smile again," said a close friend who watched the ambulance take the surviving family members to the hospital. The fire broke out at about 7pm on Christmas Eve in the property at the Jacklin family home of 2239 Iyanough Avenue, causing the death of well-known local businessman, Roscoe Jacklin. Firefighters from Hyannis FD and Yarmouth FD were still trying to smother the flames at 10.30am yesterday. When fire units arrived at the Jacklins' home, they found the three-story wood-frame house ablaze. "Flames were shooting out from all sides of the house," said Fire Chief Francis J. Boinski. Mrs. Jacklin's daughter, Alice, remains hospitalized in a satisfactory condition with first-degree burns, lacerations and possible fractures. Four investigators from the state fire marshal's office have been sifting through the remains of the home to determine the cause of the blaze. "We're sure it had something to do with the Christmas tree," Boinski said. "It had been in the home for two weeks and we believe the baseboard heating had dried it to flash-point." Mrs. Jacklin is being taken care of by a neighbour.

Morton stared at the screen. Something didn't add up. He pulled out the third and final letter that his father had written and scanned through the text. *They blame me, so I'm staying with a friend from college. He's lending me everything—I have nothing left. The truth is out, it's all over. I don't know what to do.* 'They blame me…' Morton muttered. He re-read the newspaper story. There had been no mention of his father, Jack, at all. Had he even been home on the night of the fire?

Morton printed out the entry, then wound slowly through the rest of the newspaper, not expecting to find further mention of his family. Just four pages from the end, he stopped. There, next to his name in the obituaries section, was a photograph of his grandfather. Morton stifled a gasp. Whatever bad thing Morton's father had discovered from the past, it couldn't soften the innate satisfaction of seeing his grandfather for the very first time. Roscoe Joseph Jacklin. Morton's biological grandfather. He adjusted the photo into a close-up and pushed his face nearer to the screen. It was a formal headshot where his grandfather was looking out past the camera with a fixed pose. Unsmiling and serious. He had a strong jawline and short dark hair. Morton placed both hands over the screen, creating a balaclava over his grandfather's face; the eyes staring back at him were his own. He printed the photograph then read the accompanying description.

Roscoe J. Jacklin, 48, of Iyanough Avenue, Hyannis Port, died Dec. 24th. A native of Boston, he was a renowned local businessman and owner of Hyannis Port Cars. Mr. Jacklin was a charter member of Cape Cod Lodge, on the Hyannis Board of Trade, Cape Cod Chamber of Commerce and was a corporation member of Cape Cod Hospital Association. During the Korean conflict, Mr. Jacklin served as a Sergeant First Class with the 2nd Reconnaissance Company of the U.S. Army. He leaves his widow, Velda Jacklin and two children.

The fact that he had two *children had at least been acknowledged in his obituary*, Morton thought, as he wound the film on to the next page. His hopes that the following editions of the paper might include further comment on the fire or its causes were in vain; he read every page of the final five editions of the month to no avail. He rewound the film and headed over to the help desk.

'Could I get the following couple of months' newspapers, please?' Morton asked.

'Sure thing,' said the man who had previously helped him.

Morton returned to his microfilm reader and re-read the printouts while he waited, hoping to find further clues to link the cause of the fire to his father. His father's sister, Alice, had been injured in the fire. She of all people must know what had occurred that night. He had tried contacting her last year, but her reply had been brutally blunt. *I have neither seen nor heard from my brother since 1976.* And that had been that. His attempts to establish further contact had been ignored. He knew from searches on the internet that she now worked as an artist in Provincetown, right on the tip of Cape Cod. Juliette was adamant that he should just waltz up to her art studio and introduce himself, but that was the police officer in her talking. He doubted very much that his reception would be as warm and welcoming as she imagined it would be.

Three film boxes were suddenly placed down on the table beside him. 'I've got you January and February,' he said with a grin. 'Plus March, just in case.'

'Thank you. Also, where would I find more information about a death in Hyannis Port in 1976?'

'You'd have to go to Barnstable Town Hall in Hyannis for that.'

Morton smiled, thanked him again and then began to thread up the next film.

He inched through every page of every edition, searching the stories, the adverts, the family notices—even the sports pages; but there had been nothing more written about the fire. Morton could only assume that the cause had been accidental and, therefore, not newsworthy. It still didn't explain why his father felt that he had been blamed for it, however. He slumped back in his chair. Should he continue searching? He looked at the clock—he had been here for four hours already and he still had one further place to go before meeting up with Juliette. It was time to leave.

Morton exited the library onto Boylston Street and jumped on the green T line subway to Government Center. He emerged above ground in the block-paved plaza of City Hall Square, grateful to be out of the stifling underground heat that he had found common to every subway in every country. He side-stepped away from the throng of pedestrians making their way out of the station. In front of him was the building containing the Boston seat of government: City Hall. Not exactly the most beautiful of buildings, Morton noted, as he strode towards it. Imposing and stark, the building was defined by great blocks of cantilevered concrete. He climbed the short flight of steps, entered through the doors and was immediately directed by a police officer to the back of a line winding its way obediently through officious airport-style security.

'Please remove your bags, belts and coats and empty your pockets,' a short policewoman yelled at the line. 'Take laptops or other electrical items *out* of your bags and place them in a separate tray.'

Morton obeyed, placing a random collection of objects into the grey tray: a leather belt that had seen much better days; a selection of British and American coinage; an old tissue laced with pocket fluff; and his mobile phone and laptop. The tray sailed along the conveyor belt and he passed through the metal detector without issue.

'Where abouts are birth certificates—vital records?' Morton asked a lady wearing a *City of Boston* cap and who looked vaguely as though she worked there.

'Next floor down,' she said robotically, pointing to an escalator behind her. 'Window two-one-eight.'

Morton took two escalators down to the basement, a chilliness rising to greet his descent. He stepped off into a quiet room with a distinctly oppressive atmosphere. Low ceilings. No windows. No furniture. Just polished red floor tiles and great hunks of unpainted concrete; he felt as though he had mistakenly walked into a prison waiting room. Between the concrete pillars he spotted numbered windows. *218 Births*. He headed over to it and peered over the granite counter to the open-plan office behind. Thick red tomes—presumably the birth records—surrounded tables of workers on every wall.

A woman with a kindly face smiled and came over to the window. 'Hi. How can I help?'

'Hello. I'm looking for my grandfather's birth certificate.'

The woman's smile grew. 'I love your accent—British, right?'

'Yep, that's right.'

'What happened to your face?'

Morton touched the bruise on his right cheek—the painful result of his most recent genealogical investigation back in England. 'I fell over,' he lied.

'Looks painful. So, was your grandfather born here in Boston?'

'Yes, that's right,' Morton answered.

The woman reached below the counter and produced a small slip of white paper. 'Fill this in with as much detail as you can and I'll go look for it, then you pay twelve dollars at the next window and collect it from window two-one-six.'

'Thank you,' Morton said, quickly scanning the form to ascertain what was required. 'Ah, there might be a problem: I don't know the names of my grandfather's parents—that was kind of what I was hoping to find out from the birth certificate.'

'That's okay—as long as you have the name and date of birth.'

He knew those details off by heart. Roscoe Joseph Jacklin, born 3rd April 1928 in Boston. He completed the form and handed it back.

'Okay, here's your payment slip. Take it to the next window and I'll be right back with the certificate.'

Morton took the green slip of paper, paid the twelve-dollar fee, then stood waiting patiently by window 216.

He pulled out his mobile and saw that he had a message from Juliette. *Hi Hubby. Hope you're having fun. Found your dad yet? I'm just entering the Charles River. Wish me luck. Xx*

Entering the Charles River? Swimming? Diving? He had absolutely no idea what she was talking about. He clicked reply. *??xx*

'Excuse me, sir?'

Morton pocketed his mobile and looked up. The lady was back. With empty hands and an apologetic expression on her face.

'There is no birth record for a Roscoe Jacklin born in 1928 in Boston. I shouldn't do it, but since you've come such a long way and all, I checked for several years either side of that date, but there's still nothing. Are you sure it was *Boston* and not any of the villages around here? We only cover the city itself.'

'I don't think so,' Morton replied. The information had come from his father's birth certificate, which had stated Roscoe's place of birth as Boston.

'Because if it was in the villages around here, you'll need to head out to our sister office in Dorchester.'

'How far away is that?'

'About a half hour out on the red T-line.'

Time he didn't have. 'Okay, thanks for your help.'

'You're welcome—good luck.'

Morton made his way towards the escalators, knowing that it wasn't luck he needed, just time and access to the right records. That his grandfather hadn't been born in Boston shouldn't have come as such a surprise; his entire search for his biological family had been a persistent challenge.

He glided up the escalator on a wave of thought, considering what his next steps might be.

Juliette was distinctly dry when they met thirty-five minutes later. He leant in and kissed her. 'Entering the Charles River?' he questioned.

'Duck Tour,' Juliette said by way of explanation.

'And that is…?'

'A tour of Boston in a bright red amphibious landing craft from the Second World War. Very interesting, too; I'm now an expert on the Boston Tea Party and the Civil War. What about you—how did you get on?'

'I'll tell you over dinner. Hungry?'

'Ravenous.'

'Do you fancy Legal Sea Foods? It comes recommended.'

'As opposed to *il*legal sea foods?' Juliette asked.

Morton laughed. 'Well, you are on honeymoon after all—I don't want you having to get your police warrant card out.'

She laughed. 'It's in my bag just in case…'

He took her hand in his. 'Come on, it's only just around the corner from here.'

They were lucky to get a table; the large restaurant on State Street was crowded when they arrived. A young Hispanic waiter directed them to a table with a view down the Long Wharf opposite and handed them each a menu.

'What can I get you guys to drink? We've got some great apple sangria on or our local beer is Sam Adams…or we've got a nice Californian red wine.'

'Sam Adams, please,' Morton ordered.

'The same for me,' Juliette added, receiving a surprised raised eyebrow from Morton. 'What? When in Rome…'

The waiter returned with the drinks and took their food order of clam chowder and lobster bake.

Juliette raised her beer. 'Cheers. Happy honeymoon, husband.'

'Happy honeymoon, wife.'

'Right, now I've got access to some alcohol, you can tell me about your day,' Juliette said.

'Ha, ha,' Morton replied, taking a deep breath, before running through his day's findings, ending with his inability to locate his grandfather's birth record.

Juliette listened attentively to his story. Then yawned. Then laughed. 'Sorry—blame the jetlag. Isn't there a census or something that would tell you where he was born?'

'Well…I *could* take another look at the 1930 and 1940 Federal Census,' he answered.

Juliette set her beer down. 'You've got until the food arrives to look. I'm sure they'll have Wi-Fi here.'

Morton grinned, took out his laptop and began to search the 1930 census for his grandfather. He started with Roscoe's full name, exact date of birth, and birth state of Massachusetts. Nothing. Then he opened the search up for all states. Nothing. Then he removed the date of birth completely. Nothing. There were no Roscoe Jacklins in the entirety of the United States in 1930. Then he just tried the surname Jacklin in the state of Massachusetts. Five hundred and forty-five results. Each would need checking in turn for possible errors. But not now—the waiter was heading their way with two bowls of clam chowder.

'Time's up,' Juliette announced. 'Anything?'

Morton shook his head as he shut down his laptop.

'Does all this affect the search for your dad?' Juliette asked. 'I mean, your grandfather possibly not being born in Boston isn't connected, is it?'

'No…I guess not…I just thought that, since we were in his home city, I would try and find out a bit about him.'

'Another mystery.'

'Indeed,' Morton agreed with a sigh.

Chapter Two

10th January 1976, Hyannis, Massachusetts, USA

Rory's Store, situated on the corner of Main and Pleasant Streets was deserted. Eleven days of relentless snow, where the temperature had struggled to climb above zero, had rendered the dusky streets particularly quiet. The proprietor, Rory McCoy—a beefy man in his late sixties—was leaning over the counter with both hands needlessly holding his glasses in place on the bridge of his nose. A dishevelled copy of the *Cape Cod Times* was open on the counter. Above him, an ancient heating system rattled hot, dry air into the store.

Harley 'Jack' Jacklin watched him in the mirror fixed into the corner of the ceiling that Rory had installed to monitor wayward employees and larcenous shoppers. Jack, handsome with a boyish face, was dressed in faded jeans and a loose-fitting white t-shirt with *Rory's* emblazoned on the breast pocket. Jack looked at his watch: 5.56. He was tired and he wanted to go home. The tumbling snow outside caught his attention, falling thick and fast. He wasn't in the right frame of mind for the slow trudge home.

'Hey, Jacklin,' Rory growled up at the mirror. 'I want that whole lot of detergent straightening out before you leave.'

Jack nodded at the mirror, ran his fingers through his short dark hair and obediently turned to the shelves in front of him. Making exaggerated movements for Rory's benefit, Jack shifted the boxes of *Tide* detergent, lining them up perfectly against the shelf edge.

He finished and moved on to the next, not quite believing that five minutes could take so long to pass. His actions were slow and deliberate, and his body was angled so that Rory could definitely see that he was working.

'Okay, home time,' Rory finally called.

Jack stifled a smile and strolled toward the counter.

Rory set his glasses down on the newspaper and ogled him. 'You think you're smart, Jacklin?' he asked.

Jack was taken aback by the question. What did that even mean? He was smart enough to get accepted to Boston University to study archaeology, but he wasn't smart enough to stay the course, which was why he was being paid two bucks an hour working for this blockhead. Jack shrugged.

Rory sniffed and shifted his weight in his chair. 'Let me tell you—you're not. You're working in a grocery store making washing powder look pretty. Do me a favour, would you? Just turn up on time, do what I ask and go home at the end of your shift.'

Jack nodded.

Rory fumbled below the counter, picked up Jack's coat and threw it at him.

Jack muttered a goodbye and headed for the door.

Outside, his anger was tempered by the instant bite of the freezing evening. Jack pulled up his collar and strode from the store. The vanilla halos from the streetlamps cast an unnatural glow over the sidewalks, as Jack's boots crunched down into the untrodden snow. He continued past a run of cars, held captive by the pertinacious weather, the temperature continuing to slide on the underbelly of the night.

A few minutes later, having not laid eyes on a single other soul, Jack pushed open the door to The Port Diner. Usually when he came here on a Saturday after work it would take a moment to find his two friends, but not today. Except for the waitress behind the counter, Laura Chipman was the only one here, sitting alone in their favourite booth overlooking Main Street.

'Hi,' Jack called over.

'Hi!' she beamed.

Jack slid across the red leather seat opposite her. 'No Michael?'

Laura shook her head. 'He's not coming—he's at our uncle's house and his car won't start and he can't be bothered to walk.'

'Oh, that's a real shame,' Jack said, crestfallen.

'Yeah, our last time together for a while,' Laura bemoaned. 'I tried to persuade him but he's got packing to do.'

'You folks ready to order?' the waitress called over.

Jack nodded and she scuttled over in her red and white outfit, pen and pad poised and ready.

'Two hot chocolates, please,' Jack ordered.

'Sure. You want whipped cream?'

The pair nodded.

'Anything else?'

'Not for me, thanks—I've got dinner waiting for me at home,' Jack replied.

'Me too,' Laura added.

'No problem,' the waitress said, before heading off to the kitchens.

'Dinner and a whole bunch of packing,' Laura grimaced.

Jack smiled. Laura was returning to Boston University tomorrow for the new semester. The same as her twin brother, Michael. The same as Jack's sister, Alice. The same as other old friends from high school. 'Looking forward to going back?'

'To the assignments, the early-morning lectures and the exams? Yeah, sure,' she laughed.

Jack grinned but knew that she was just being kind. She loved it at college, thrived on it. She had an amazing future in front of her. Unlike him. His future looked barren, stagnant. A slow death in a small-town grocery store.

'How was work?' Laura asked.

'Awesome,' Jack began enthusiastically. 'I filled shelves *all* day. It was just the best. Cans of meat. Cans of fish. Soap powder. I even got to fill up the sale bin. Toilet tissue, sixty-nine cents. Mayonnaise, fifty-nine cents. Trash bags, eighty-nine cents.'

Laura rolled her eyes.

'I know—I've only got myself to blame,' Jack lamented, intuiting her gentle condemnation. 'I should have stayed on at school.'

'Was it really *so* bad?' Laura asked.

Jack shrugged. 'I love archaeology and history but it just wasn't enough about the people for me—you know? Too much on artefacts rather than who used them.'

'Maybe you didn't give it long enough?' she ventured. 'You barely made one semester, after all.'

Jack thought about her question. She might have been right and he had quitted too soon. He guessed he would never know; now his passion for history and people and his high grades at school were being used to ensure boxes of detergent were correctly aligned.

'Here you go,' the waitress said, setting the tray down on the table between them. 'Two hot chocolates with extra cream. Enjoy.'

They both thanked her and she returned to her position behind the counter, staring out at the deserted street.

Jack removed his jacket, warm blood finally creeping back to his extremities. He cupped his hot chocolate with both hands and he met Laura's dark eyes. She was pretty—he'd always thought it and people were always telling her so—but she was too demure, too self-effacing to accept it.

'What?' Laura questioned.

'Nothing,' Jack answered. 'Just thinking I'll miss you when you're gone—and Michael, of course.'

'We'll be back in no time—you'll see.'

He nodded, but her words curdled with his belief about their future. She and Michael would become ever more fulfilled by their time at Boston University and his time with them—these simple hot chocolates, or milkshakes in the summer—would come to mean ever less until they had nothing left in common but the drinks on the table in front of them.

'Come on, Jack—stop being so miserable—it's my last night on the Cape,' Laura chided.

'Sorry…' Jack mumbled.

'What have you got planned for the next couple of days?' she asked.

Tomorrow was Sunday. He would be helping his dad with household chores. Then it was back to the store on Monday. Repeat. Day after day. 'Nothing special.'

He raised his mug of hot chocolate, downed it in one go, then stood up and pulled on his coat. Fumbling in his pocket, he placed a dollar bill and a fifteen-cent tip down on the table. 'I have to go—Mom will be wondering where I am. Take care getting off the Cape tomorrow.'

'Is that it?' Laura called after him. 'Wait—at least give me a hug goodbye.'

Jack paused and turned to face her; the self-directed biliousness that he had inadvertently vented at his friend dissolved. Jack was certain that their friendship was on the precipice of permanent change, but he wasn't going to be the one to end it. Not here. Not today. He walked over to Laura with an apologetic smile and pulled her into a tight embrace, his fingers touching the soft strands of her mousey hair. 'Sorry.'

'Okay, you're suffocating me now!' Laura exclaimed.

Jack released her and took her left hand in his. 'Take care, okay? And write me.'

Laura leant over and kissed him on the cheek. 'Bye, Jack.'

'Bye,' he replied. He paced to the door without looking back.

Jack finally reached his street. The usual forty-five-minute walk to Iyanough Avenue had already taken him more than an hour. In places, the snow had risen above his knees and walking had felt like wading through a lake of maple syrup. Here, however, just yards from Hyannis Harbor, the fresh falling snow had failed to battle against the coarse saline winds that rose from the North Atlantic, endowing the sidewalks with just a thin translucent glaze.

He looked out at the harbour, usually peppered with the tiny lights of expensive moored yachts. Tonight, there was nothing out there but snowflakes frenetically dancing in the grey.

Jack neared his parents' house. The soft ochre lights from inside demarked it, pulling the white timber-clad structure from the monochrome background. He stepped onto the veranda and unlocked the door. A breath of appreciatively warm air, laced with the smells of his mom's cooking, brushed over him as he stepped inside.

'Dinner's ready, Jack,' his mom called out from the kitchen.

Jack hung up his coat, removed his boots and followed the scented trail into the kitchen where he found his mom, dad and sister sitting at the table. Their dinners were untouched and their silent eyes were fixed upon him as he walked towards them.

Jack took his usual place opposite his sister, Alice.

'Lord, bless this food and family,' his dad said quietly. He smiled and picked up his knife and fork.

'Did something keep you from making it home on time?' his mom asked.

'Sorry,' Jack murmured. 'The snow was real deep in places, it was—'

'I expect you found time to meet your friends, though,' his dad interrupted.

'Only for five minutes.'

His dad nodded, emitting a noise of satisfaction.

From the corner of his eye, Jack studied his dad. In his late forties, he was losing the fight to middle-age; his combed-over hair was greying and thin and the lines around his eyes and forehead were now permanently shadowed gullies. He was punctiliously dissecting the slab of pork on his plate, mixing it with a small quantity of carrot and boiled potato. There was a rhythmical cadence to his eating. Every meal was the same.

A sharp pain struck Jack's shin bone. He stifled a yelp and scowled at Alice. A quick flick of her head, and an agitated gesture of her eyes towards his plate, made him realise that he had completely stopped eating and was gaping at his dad like a stunned goldfish. He lowered his gaze to his own plate and quickly took a slice of pork.

'So, honey—just like I said I would, I found someone to take away those old boxes from the basement for you.'

'Oh, that's wonderful,' his mom chirped, clearly delighted.

'Yeah, a guy who runs the antique store up in Dennis.'

'What boxes?' Jack enquired.

His mom rolled her eyes. 'Old boxes of junk that have been taking up far too much space for far too long.'

'He's going to swing by tomorrow and take a look. He says he'll give a fair price.'

'Well, that sure is great,' Velda concurred. 'I think we could open up an antiques store with all we've accumulated over the years.'

'What about you, Alice?' Roscoe asked. 'Are you all fired up and ready to go back to college tomorrow? Get behind the easel again?'

'Yes—I can't wait. This semester is print-making and ceramics.'

'That sure sounds exciting,' Roscoe replied. 'We'll leave after breakfast—hopefully give the sun and the snow-ploughs a chance to clear the roads so we can get off the Cape.'

After dessert, Jack headed upstairs to his room, closing the door behind him. He sank down onto his bed and stared up at the ceiling, wondering what he could do to breach this wall of stagnation that had imperceptibly risen around him, preventing access to any alternative life to that which he was now living. Reaching across to the top drawer of his bedside table, he removed a photograph and held it above him. He thought for a moment then realised that the picture had been taken almost exactly two years ago. It was of him and his one and only girlfriend, Margaret Farrier. They were standing outside her house on Canterbury Road, Folkestone in England, their fingers timidly entwined and shy grins etched on their faces.

Jack lowered the picture, bringing Margaret just inches from his face. *Why did you stop writing to me?* he wondered. His letters—almost one a month since the visit to England—had gone unanswered. All except for one reply. She had been, and still was, his only relationship, so he had had little with which he could compare it, but it had felt to him as though they had had something special together. He had been naïve, he realised now, to think that their relationship could have survived the three-thousand-mile gulf between them. Stupid. He reached over and pulled out the single letter that he had received from her. *18th January 1974. Dear Jack, Thank you so much for your letter. Glad the flight home was good. I'm missing you, too! I think it was one of the best weeks of my life. Yes, I suppose I am your girlfriend now! I've already told my dad that I want to get a job so I can start saving to come and see you, but I don't have a clue how much it costs to fly to America! I didn't tell him how close we have become, but* *he wasn't happy that I was 'frequenting' with you at all. I'm not sure what upset him most—that you're American or that you're FOUR years older than me! I'm sure if my mum had been alive, she would have been more understanding. She must have been in love with my dad at some point...* He held the letter close to his nose. For a while—the first few days—the letter had carried a faint echo of her scent: the sweet citrusy fragrance of her perfume, laced over the dry tobacco smell from her father's pipes that he recalled had pervaded their home. The peculiar aroma had slowly faded, and now it smelt of nothing at all.

His meandering thoughts of Margaret snapped like a twig when Alice tapped on his door. He knew that it was her from the light *tap, tap, tap,* that she always did. He hastily shoved the letter and photograph back into the drawer then called: 'Come in.'

Alice stepped in and pushed the door closed behind her. He could tell that she was anxious about something; her eyes always gave her away. They were chestnut brown—just like his but more striking, somehow. He could always tell if he'd annoyed or upset her, just from a quick look into her eyes.

'What's up?' he asked, drawing his knees to his chest.

'You,' she answered, sitting in the space where his feet had been.

'Me?'

Alice ran her fingers through her thick curly hair and faced him. 'I've got a plan,' she said, taking a long, dramatic breath. 'You come with me back to college—get yourself a job in the city someplace—until you figure out what it is that you want to do with your life. You can sleep on the floor in my room until you get yourself sorted out.' She stood up and added: 'Come on, I'll help you pack.'

Jack reached out, grabbed her hand and pulled her back down beside him. 'It's real sweet of you, Ali, but no; I can't.'

'Why not?' she said, her eyes conveying her disappointment.

'I can't just run away like that. I need to stay here and figure things out.' He placed a hand in between her shoulder blades. 'I'll be okay—really. I'm twenty, for God's sake!'

'And what—you're going to live here forever?' she jibed.

'Probably,' Jack answered with a laugh.

'What are you going to do tonight?' Alice asked. 'Come downstairs and watch *M*A*S*H*?'

'I think I'll pass.'

'You mean you don't want to hear Dad's *it-wasn't-actually-like-that-in-Korea* comments?'

'Tempting, but no. I'll read for a bit then get an early night.'

'Me too—once I've finished packing.' Alice stood and made for the door.

'Thanks for coming in,' Jack said.

'I was serious, you know.'

She was serious, too; again, her eyes said so. He nodded and watched her leave. Then he lay back down, placing his hands behind his head, as his thoughts returned to his time in England with Margaret.

The next morning, the house was filled with mildly chaotic activity. The snow had stopped falling at some point in the night and the sun was pushing through the kitchen window, harsh and bright. Jack was sitting at the breakfast table, sipping coffee while his sister, mom and dad flapped around the place preparing to get Alice back to Boston. His dad was loading the car; Alice was finalising her packing and his mom was hauling yet another tray of cakes out of the oven.

Not for the first time that morning, Jack's gaze had fallen onto the five storage boxes lined up neatly by the kitchen door. At first, when his dad had brought them up from the basement, Jack had presumed that they were going to Boston with Alice. But then his dad had revealed that they were the boxes of junk awaiting collection.

Several minutes later, after Jack had said goodbye to his sister, he took advantage of the opportunity of his mom waving them off to take a look inside the boxes.

He peered inside the first one—the only one labelled 'private' and removed a bundle of official-looking papers. Certificates and insurances, by the looks of things. He thumbed through the stack, pausing briefly with each new document. Why on earth his parents were getting rid of such important paperwork was a mystery. He continued flicking through tax and car records, stopping suddenly at an official-looking certificate. He caught sight of his dad's name.

'What's that you've got there?' his mom asked, suddenly appearing in the kitchen.

Jack quickly concertinaed the papers back together. 'Are you sure you want to get rid of these? They seem pretty important, if you ask me.'

'Oh my goodness!' she said, snatching the papers and placing them back inside the box. She carried it to the other side of the room, muttering as she went. 'Your dad—honestly.'

'Do you want me to take it back down to the basement for you?' Jack suggested, wanting to get another look at what he had just seen.

'Oh, no—I'll do that. But you could check the rest of the boxes for me—make sure your dad didn't bring any others up that he shouldn't have.'

Jack knelt beside the other boxes. As he removed the lids, he tried to recall what he had just seen among the official family paperwork. The isolated words that he had glimpsed before his mom had derailed his thoughts didn't make any sense.

'Are they the right ones?' Velda asked.

Jack looked inside them. 'Yeah, I think so,' he answered, picking through an assortment of items: candlesticks, old picture frames and a selection of unsightly ornaments. Opening the final box, he asked, 'What's all this?' He carefully withdrew the contents, setting them down on the kitchen floor. Medals. Bullets. A leather map case. Dog tags. Ammunition pouches. A watch. A bayonet and scabbard.

'Just old family stuff—my dad's old war junk,' Velda said, barely flicking her eyes in his direction. 'Stuff that belongs in the past.'

He removed the last item from the box—a First World War Colt M1909 handgun—and held it in his hands, slowly rotating it around and examining it in detail. As he looked down the scarred barrel, his mind began to slip into the imagined history of his grandfather's war holding this very weapon. It fell to the fantasy of his mind to recreate the scene, for his mom and dad had always refused to be drawn on their family's past. He didn't even know in which theatre of war his grandfather had served. 'Mom, what do you know about your dad's time in the war?' he tried again.

'Oh, goodness, not more questions about the past. He died in the winter of the Great Depression, Jack, when I was three. What he did in the war is anyone's guess.'

'Did your mom never speak of it?' Jack pushed.

'No.'

'Don't you want to know more about your ancestors?'

'No, I really don't,' Velda said firmly. 'The past is in the past—let's leave it there, shall we.'

Jack continued to examine the artefacts, as his mom busied herself with the mountain of washing up that had risen from her baking efforts this morning.

The doorbell rang. 'I'll go,' she said. 'It'll be Betty calling to collect me for church.'

As his mom trundled to the front door, muttering something about Betty's being far too early, Jack rushed over to the box containing the private papers. He quickly opened it and flicked through to the piece of paper that he had either imagined that he had seen, or that didn't correlate at all with his known narrative of his family's past. He found the certificate but had no time to read it: his mom's voice at the door, brief and surprised, revealed that she was heading back inside.

'Jack—it's Laura,' she called.

Jack pocketed the certificate, set the lid down in place and strolled casually into the hallway, where he passed his mom. 'Laura. What are you doing here?'

'Well that sure is a nice greeting,' she teased.

Jack reached the front door, perplexed to see her. Whatever the reason for her visit, it was fleeting, for her red Plymouth Barracuda was parked up outside, the engine still running. 'Sorry, I wasn't expecting you.'

'It's a flying visit. My dad wants to see you.'

'Your dad? Why? What have I done?' Jack asked.

'He's got a job offer for you,' she revealed in a hushed voice.

'Oh. Doing what?'

'You'll have to wait and see. He's expecting you today. Bye,' she said, leaning in and kissing him on the cheek.

Jack, slightly dumbstruck, watched her jog back down the steps, then give a little wave as she climbed into her car and drove off. He looked out over Hyannis Harbor, wondering what on earth sort of job her father could be going to offer him. As far as Jack was aware, he had been retired for several years. 'Mom, I'm going out. See you later.'

Once clear of the house, Jack pulled the document from his pocket. It was a marriage certificate.

He read it meticulously several times, but each reading added nothing to his understanding.

Chapter Three

15th August 2016, Hyannis Port, Massachusetts, USA

Morton killed the engine of the hire car, silencing the whir of the air conditioning. He stepped out into a strange stillness that pervaded Iyanough Avenue, observing the run of exclusive detached homes that lined the water front. Each was distinctly different from the next, but all were cladded in white or grey weatherboarding and each came with an unobstructed view of Hyannis Harbor—now bustling with small private yachts. He had parked the car on a grass verge close to the driveway of 2239—the house in which his father had resided until his disappearance in 1976.

Morton took out his mobile phone and took a series of photographs of the house and the street, then ducked his head back inside the car. 'Wish me luck.'

'Good luck,' Juliette said.

Morton strolled up towards the house as casually as he could, but inside he was trying to work out exactly what he was going to say. He hadn't figured it out by the time he had pressed the doorbell.

The door was opened quickly by a middle-aged man in a shirt, jeans and bare feet. 'Hi,' he greeted.

'Hi, sorry to disturb you,' Morton began, hurriedly removing his sunglasses. 'I'm looking for—'

'The Kennedy Compound?' the man interjected. 'It's just at the end of this street, but unless you're a *very* good friend of theirs, you're not even going to get a glimpse of the place. Your best bet—'

It was Morton's turn to interrupt. 'No, I'm not looking for the Kennedys—I'm looking for my father—he lived here in 1976—the year it burnt down…'

'Oh, I see—forgive me—I thought you were another Kennedy tourist. People see the Kennedy house marked on Google maps and think that they can just drive right up to it and knock on the door. Sorry. So your dad lived here, you say huh?'

'Yes, that's right. I was just wondering if you had any information about the fire, what happened, or…?' As soon as the words were out of his mouth, Morton realised how silly they sounded. 'I know it's a long shot,' he added.

The man shook his head. 'We moved here back in 1994. I mean the place was completely rebuilt before we even got here.' He stepped to one side. 'You're welcome to come take a look around, but there's literally *nothing* of the original house left. From what I can gather it was razed to the ground.'

'No, it's okay—thank you. I knew it wasn't very likely, but thought it was worth a try.'

'Didn't someone die in the fire?' the man asked.

'Yeah, my grandfather—my father disappeared soon afterwards and now I'm trying to find him.'

'Wow—you've sure got your work cut out. I just don't have anything here that relates to the old house—not even any old paperwork or anything.'

'I didn't really expect that you would,' Morton acknowledged.

'I'm just trying to think if there's anyone in the neighbourhood who was here back then and there's just nobody that I can think of, sorry. The neighbours on either side of us are all relatively new.'

'Don't worry—thanks for your time, though. I'll leave you to it.'

'Okay. Well, I hope you find the answers you're looking for.'

Morton ambled slowly down the drive, absorbing his surroundings. He paused before he climbed into the car, taking in the view before him—exactly the same view as his father would have seen every day until he vanished forty years ago. He turned back to the house and imagined it as it would have been on that fateful Christmas Eve. Snow on the ground. Darkness but for the flames eating the house from the inside out. His father watching the building collapse. His grandfather trapped inside. What happened next? Morton knew that his father had gone to stay with a friend in the next street, from where he had written his final letter to Morton's mother. It was time to go and visit that house.

'No joy?' Juliette asked, as he climbed back into the car and fired up the engine.

'No—they don't know anything. He said I could go inside and take a look around, but what's the point? I might as well look in any old random place on the street.'

'Where to now?'

'Ocean Avenue—not far away.'

'Where your dad stayed after the fire?'

'Yep.'

It took less than two minutes to get there. As Morton swung into the drive, he knew he was in for another disappointment. The house was crippled by years—possibly decades—of abandonment. Among the wild undergrowth rose a broad grey three-storey building. On the floor around it were puddles of smashed glass, the open cavities an access point for a range of vermin now treating this place as home. Something—whether deliberate or natural—had torn a large hole in the roof, exposing the inside to further destruction.

'Looks like the owner might be out,' Juliette quipped.

Morton shot her a strong look. 'I'll just have a peek inside.'

'*Please* don't,' she begged, 'I can't save you over here.'

It was a fair point; she had come to his rescue on multiple occasions back in England. 'I'll be two minutes,' he promised. 'And I won't leave your sight.'

'Just to warn you—I won't pay the bail.'

Morton grinned, closed the car door and walked up the steps to the porch. He tried the front door. Locked, though God only knew why; anyone with the remotest inclination could easily have gained access. He peered through a narrow, glass-less window beside the door. As expected, the inside was dilapidated, ripped apart and, in places, burned. If he'd been alone, he would have climbed inside, just to see it for himself, to stand on the very floorboards upon which his father had also once stood.

He stepped from the porch and looked at the upstairs rooms. His father had slept up there, somewhere. But whose house was this? And where did his father go from here? This ramshackle building was his final clue. He stared at the house and, for the first time since leaving England, doubt crept into his mind. They were on honeymoon for three weeks, but with the final week being spent in New York. That gave him just one week and six days to find his father. A massive challenge, now that he was actually here, facing yet more setbacks.

'I'll find you,' he whispered under his breath, turning from the house back towards the car. He climbed in and added the next destination to the GPS: Oak Neck Cemetery. Four minutes.

'What's there?' Juliette asked. 'Or *who's* there, should I say?'

'My grandfather—possibly my grandmother, too, for all I know,' he replied, pulling out onto the quiet back streets of Hyannis Port.

The sprawling green lawns of Oak Neck Cemetery spilled down to meet the roadside. Morton drew the car to a stop and they both climbed out. The cemetery was large but the gravestones were sporadic, which didn't bode well for him. In England, a sparsely memorialised cemetery was usually an indication that below the perfect lawns were thousands of unmarked graves.

'You take that half in the sun and I'll take this half in the shade?' Juliette suggested with a smile.

'Done. Remember—any Jacklin graves at all—give me a shout.'

He watched with a pang of tenderness, as Juliette made for the first memorials, seeming to float in her white summer dress and floppy straw hat. He really was a lucky man to have married her.

He turned to the first headstone. *Dolloff*, large letters shouted from the top of the granite. That was one good thing about modern American headstones—there was no need to get right up close in order to determine the name of the deceased. He moved along past a large pine tree to the next two stones. *Clark* and *Walton*, both replete with small American flags. Then he moved to the next row. Five more graves—none of them correct.

He wiped the sweat from his brow and marched along the next line. There were more graves here, but none for which he was searching.

'Morton!'

He turned to see Juliette waving frantically at him. She pointed animatedly to the grave beside her. 'Look!' She'd found it. Despite the debilitating heat, he ran towards her. He reached her and glanced at the nearby graves. There was something he clearly wasn't getting. 'Isn't that a funny name? Geoffrey S. Skull—Geoffrey's Skull?'

'Is that it?'

'It's funny,' Juliette defended.

'Hmm,' Morton mumbled humourlessly, as he walked back to continue his search.

More rows of graves with names other than that for which he searched.

Then, a few minutes later, Juliette called out again. 'Here.'

'Is it his headstone or another funny one?' Morton shouted before he bothered to traipse over to her.

'It's his—Roscoe Jacklin.'

Morton didn't run this time, but, even before he got close to her, he could see the name etched into a low gravestone: Jacklin.

'It's him,' Juliette repeated, as he reached her. 'Your grandfather.'

Morton drew a quick breath and crouched down in front of the light grey granite stone. Below the word Jacklin was carved his grandfather's name. *1928 Roscoe J. 1976.*

'There's space for another name to be added,' Juliette noted.

Morton nodded his agreement. Did that mean that his grandmother was still alive?

Then he spotted something at the foot of the grave. He picked it up and examined it. A shrivelled up white rose. Someone still visited the grave, he reasoned. Just not very often, by the looks of it. 'What do you think? Two weeks old? Three?'

'Somewhere around there, yes. It could have been put there by your Aunt Alice,' Juliette suggested, intuiting his thoughts.

'Could be, but it's a bit of a trek down from Provincetown,' Morton pondered. He wanted to allow at least for the slim possibility that the rose might have been placed here by his father.

'Let me take a photo of you beside the grave,' Juliette suggested.

Morton manoeuvred himself behind the grave and crouched down. Never really certain of the etiquette for cemetery photo shoots, Morton offered a vague half-smile, then took the camera from Juliette and took some of his own photos to add to his growing file on his paternal family tree.

'Bye, Grandad or Grandpa or whatever I might have called you,' he said, touching the top of the warm granite before taking Juliette's hand and heading back to the car.

'Are you sure you don't mind?' Morton asked, as they stepped from the Green Lotus Café on Hyannis Main Street.

Seemingly from thin air, Juliette produced her credit card. 'All the while I have *this* and all of *these*—' then she gestured to the long line of shops on either side of the wide road '—then I'm happy. You take as long as you need.' She pecked him on the lips, twirled around and began down the street.

'I'll phone you when I'm done,' Morton called after her.

She waved her credit card and continued to walk.

Morton grinned as he tracked her for half a block, then turned in beside the bustling JFK Museum. At the end of a long path that bisected a perfect lawn was an official-looking brick building. The sign beside the entrance read *Barnstable Town Hall, 367 Main Street.* He climbed the steps and, once inside, paused, searching for an indication of where to go. A piece of paper stuck to the wall had a big red arrow under the words *Town Clerk's Office. Dog licenses. Marriage licenses. Birth certificates. Death certificates. Business certificates. Voter registration. And numerous other things.*

Just the place.

He strode down the corridor, in through a grey door and found himself in an open-plan office.

'What can I get you?' a lady yapped from her desk nearby. She had the jet-black hair and olive skin of someone freshly delivered from the Mediterranean.

'Hi, I'm looking for information on a death in Hyannis Port in 1976.'

The woman nodded. 'I'll be right back.' The woman ambled off through a door at the rear of the room.

Morton took his pen and notepad from his bag and waited patiently. Moments later, she shuffled back towards him and dropped a black leather-bound book on the counter between them. 'Here you go,' she said.

'Thank you.' Morton delved eagerly into the ledger. He swiftly flicked through several pages until he reached December, then he began carefully running his finger down the surnames until he found his grandfather.

Name: Roscoe Joseph Jacklin
Sex: Male
Colour: White
Condition: Married
Age: 48 years, 8 months, 21 days
Disease or cause of death: Accidental death resulting from extensive burns
Residence: Hyannis Port
Place of burial: Old Neck
Occupation: Businessman
Place of birth: Boston
Name and birthplace of father: George P. Jacklin, Boston
Name and birthplace of mother: Lucy Bradford, Boston

He quickly scribbled the new information onto his notepad. He now knew the names of his great-grandparents. 'Excuse me,' he called over to the clerk.

'Yes.'

'I found who I was looking for—is there any further information—like a death certificate that I can get from this?'

'Sure.' She stood up, took a piece of paper from under the desk and passed it across the counter. 'Fill this in, and the certificate's all yours for ten dollars,' she said with a wink.

Morton hurriedly completed the form and handed it back with a ten-dollar bill.

'I'll be right back.'

And in the time that it took for Morton to begin to attach imagined lives to the names of his great-grandparents, she was back. She handed him an A4 sheet of paper with the embossed seal of Barnstable Town on the bottom. He thanked her and stepped to the side of the room to read its contents. The certificate confirmed everything that the index had just told him, including his grandfather's parents' names, but with some additional information: the name of the funeral home and funeral director was stated, as was the fact that he had been a veteran of the Korean conflict. The informant of the death had been his wife, Velda Jacklin, and she had confirmed that his place of birth had been Boston.

Morton carefully folded the certificate into his bag and made his way out of the Town Hall. He found an empty bench in the welcome shade of a large maple tree. Pulling open his laptop, he ran a Google search for *Grant Funeral Home*. Thankfully, they were still in business. He emailed them a brief summary of what he was looking for and clicked send.

Next, he opened the 1930 Federal Census and ran a search for his great-grandfather, George P. Jacklin and his wife, Lucy. One result. In San Francisco, California. Three thousand miles from Boston. He opened the page and instantly saw why his grandfather had not shown up in previous searches: he was listed as Joseph Jacklin—not Roscoe. There were two other children in the house: John and David Jacklin.

Morton considered what he had just discovered. His grandmother, Velda had evidently believed that her husband had been born in Boston, Massachusetts, yet clearly he had not been. *Why would his grandfather tell his wife that he had been born on the other side of the country?* Morton wondered. Did this have anything to do with his father's disappearance?

He needed to see if there were more records in California pertaining to his grandfather. Navigating through the Ancestry website, he typed in Joseph Jacklin's name, along with those of his parents. One suggested record matched the search criteria: a marriage on the 4th

March 1949 in San Francisco, between Joseph Jacklin and Audrey Fuller.

Morton studied the entry for some time. Four years after this marriage, Joseph—under the name Roscoe—had married Velda Henderson in Wellfleet, Massachusetts, stating himself to be a bachelor. The implication was clear; that Velda had no knowledge of her husband's birth and marriage three thousand miles away in California.

As he had done several times in the past few months, Morton allowed his mind to ramble back to an imagined scene of his grandparents' wedding on Cape Cod. Only this time, thanks to the newspaper report of the fire, his grandfather's face had sharpened into focus. His grandmother, Velda, was still a blur, yet still Morton felt a deep sympathy for her marrying a man with a clearly secretive past.

Morton wanted to know more about that life, becoming more convinced that it could have a bearing on his father's disappearance.

Opening up the 1940 Federal Census, he searched again for his grandfather—this time under the name Joseph with parents George and Lucy. He found them easily. They were living in a house on Russian Hill, San Francisco. Before he could read the finer detail about his family, he was distracted by a familiar name in the neighbouring house. Living next door to his twelve-year-old grandfather was his eleven-year-old grandmother, Velda Henderson, with her sister and widowed mother.

Morton stared at the screen as the fictional scenes that he had created once again collided with hard genealogical facts. His grandmother had to have known her husband's place of birth and probably also, therefore, of his previous marriage.

'What were you both running from?' Morton murmured.

Chapter Four

4th March 1949, Cow Hollow, San Francisco, California, USA

Velda Henderson was shaking. She hadn't noticed it until she looked at herself in her full-length bedroom mirror. Her hands were quivering as if she had some peculiar illness. She clasped them together and steadied them on her stomach. She needed to calm down before she left the house, but time was running out—she literally had one hour until it was all too late. Her heart, though, told her that it already was, but still the demons inside her mind persisted.

Closing her eyes, she pictured calmness as a physical entity; she imagined a viscous liquid akin to blood slowly seeping through the blackness of her body. She dragged the breath in and out of her lungs, as though it were a great effort.

When she opened her eyes minutes later she was composed. The shaking had stopped. She smiled, took a step back and regarded herself in the mirror. Perfect. She was wearing a brand-new dress in the 'New Look' style—padded hips, rounded shoulders and a wasp waist. It was white with a blue and red swirling pattern that would have been completely unimaginable just four years ago what with the depravations of war. To complete the look, she wore ostrich platform shoes that gave perfect definition to her legs. Quite what her mother would have made of such an outfit was anyone's guess.

With an extravagant twirl, she opened her bedroom door and descended the staircase to the large entrance hall below. Her sister and some of their mutual friends were scattered around the house, getting themselves ready for the wedding in just under forty-five minutes' time.

It was now or never.

She quietly slipped from the house and walked a short distance up the steep incline, then stopped. She glanced up at the imposing house that was next door to hers; the tiny voice inside her that said that this wasn't a good idea made one final plea.

With the thinnest veil of confidence, she climbed the stairs and rang the bell.

'Velda! Come on in.' It was David, Joseph's younger brother and best man. He stepped to one side and she entered the house. 'He's up in his room—pacing the floor by the sounds of it.'

'Thank you,' Velda replied, taking some meaning from the fact that Joseph seemed anxious. She climbed the stairs and crossed the upstairs hallway to his bedroom. She paused for a moment then tapped lightly on the door.

'Yes,' Joseph called.

There was a hint of annoyance or displeasure, Velda noted, as she entered the room. 'Hi, Joseph.'

He was sitting on the edge of his bed, his elbows on his knees, his head in his hands. 'Velda—I wasn't expecting to see you at the wedding today, much less appear in my room right before it.' He stood up and faced her.

'I had to see you,' she said quietly. 'I need to tell you something.'

Joseph's head sank down in a sigh. 'Velda, listen—'

'She's not really pregnant,' Velda blurted.

Joseph looked up, startled. 'How did you know she *was* pregnant?' he whispered.

'That doesn't matter—what matters is that it's the reason you're marrying her, isn't it?'

Joseph paused and glared at her before answering. 'It's much more complicated than that.'

'Well, she's not pregnant—so if that's your only reason for marrying her...then you don't need to now.'

'How do you know she's *not* pregnant?'

Velda shrugged. 'She told her friend, Rachel.'

Joseph emitted a mock laugh. 'And let me guess, Rachel told her sister, who told your sister, who told you—that it?' Joseph demanded.

'Why does it matter how I found out? What matters is she's lying and she's only saying it so that you marry her...and not...' Velda's words ran dry in her mouth.

'You? Jesus, Velda. And what—you thought *we'd* get married instead? We've not been together for months now—long before Audrey even came along.'

'Three weeks before Audrey came along—apparently.'

'So what, you're saying that I was dating her behind your back?' he fumed. 'Have you heard yourself, Velda? This is—what, thirty minutes before my wedding? I guess you want me to thank you? Well, thanks for the information.'

Hot, unstoppable tears began to moisten Velda's eyes as she searched for something that she could say to prevent, change or soften the inevitable that was about to occur, but every scenario ended the same: the demise of their relationship.

The tears finally broke free at the same time as Joseph's bedroom door was flung wide open.

'Time to go, buddy,' David said. 'You okay, Velda?'

Velda managed to shake her head, then she made a run for the open door.

'See you at the wedding,' Joseph called after her.

She ran out of the house, but instead of turning back towards her own place, she headed out in the opposite direction. She hastily removed her shoes, discarding them where they fell, and ran. The demons were speaking more loudly now, pushing her past the point where her lungs ached for air and begged her to slow down.

She stopped and stared. The intricate thoughts that were woven through her mind suddenly began to separate, like a rope being unravelled into its individual strands. Just in front of her was the Golden Gate Bridge. The place where her mother had committed suicide four years previously.

Velda walked towards the bridge, her mind beginning to clear.

Chapter Five

11th January 1976, Hyannis Port, Massachusetts, USA

The Chipman house—a ten-minute walk away on Ocean Avenue—was a place that Jack had seldom visited, despite knowing Laura and Michael for five years since they had moved to Hyannis Port from Alberta in Canada. The house was, by anyone's standards, in need of some heavy-duty maintenance, which was why, he guessed, Laura and Michael rarely invited him over. Right now, Jack thought, as he approached the front door, it looked like the perfect location for a horror movie. He pressed the doorbell and waited, half expecting the door to creak slowly open and some fiendish butler to gawk out at him.

However, the door was noiselessly opened by Laura and Michael's father. He stood with a wide grin, an otherwise imposing figure in dishevelled shabby clothes and with a monstrously long and tangled beard.

'Mr Chipman,' Jack began, 'Laura said that you—'

'Yes, yes, wait there,' Mr Chipman cut in. He disappeared momentarily into the gloom of the house, returning moments later carrying a bunch of keys. 'Let's go.'

'Where are we going?' Jack asked.

'To find Hope,' he replied, leading the way around the back of the house to his 1940s green Chrysler Saratoga. 'Get in.'

Despite the bizarreness of the situation, Jack obeyed and sat beside Mr Chipman, not relishing the stench of fried food and engine oil that permeated the old car.

'So, Laura tells me that you hate your job at the grocery store—that right?' Mr Chipman quizzed, as he began their journey.

'Yeah,' Jack admitted. It was somehow okay for him to vocalise the truth to Laura and Michael, but, for some reason it felt like an admission of failure when he said it to someone of his parents' generation. 'It's not going so well.'

Mr Chipman nodded, gently tugged on his beard and continued pushing the car northwards, through the snow-ploughed roads towards Barnstable. Quite where he could be taking him and what kind of employment he might be offered totally baffled Jack.

'And what is it you'd like to do, exactly?' Mr Chipman asked.

There was a question. Jack looked out of his window for a moment and thought. 'History. People.'

Mr Chipman chuckled. 'Good answer.'

Jack was confused; it had been a terrible answer. True, but terrible.

Mr Chipman changed the subject. He spoke about Laura and Michael. He spoke about the weather. He spoke about politics. Then he suddenly swung the car off-road and switched off the ignition.

Jack looked around them. They were parked beside a low stone wall, partially covered by giant drifts of snow. He craned his neck and spotted some graves. They were outside a cemetery.

Mr Chipman stared at Jack for a moment, then smiled, as if Jack should somehow be able to intuit the reason for their being here. 'Follow me.'

Jack climbed from the car and spotted a simple white plaque on a wooden frame. *Lothrop Hill Cemetery.* It still made no sense.

Jack followed in Mr Chipman's footsteps as they tramped through ankle-deep dunes of snow, through the open gate and into the cemetery. Rectangles of faded grey headstones broke through the blanket of otherwise unblemished white. A northern cardinal, stark red, was sitting atop one of the graves, watching as they slogged further into the grounds.

Mr Chipman suddenly came to a halt and crossed his arms.

Jack spotted the curious expression on his face that left him with the distinct impression that there was something that he clearly wasn't getting. Jack searched around him, certain that he was missing something obvious. Then he spotted it. A grave with a familiar name. *Hope Chipman.* Finding Hope; now he understood. Sort of. Jack leant in closer to the grave and wiped a light dusting of snow from the ancient lettering. *Here lyeth interred ye body of Mrs Hope Chipman ye wife of Elder John Chipman aged 54 years who changed this life for a better ye 8 of January 1683.* 'So she was born in 1629—one of the first settlers?' Jack proposed. 'And one of your ancestors?'

'Precisely!' Mr Chipman said, a note of triumphant pride in his voice. 'My eight times great-grandmother. She was born in the Plymouth colony. Her father was John Howland—one of the *Mayflower* pilgrims.'

'You're lucky,' Jack commented, 'I don't even know who my grandparents were...'

'Well, I can always help you with that,' Mr Chipman offered. 'That is, if you'll accept my offer of employment?'

Jack looked curiously at him. 'What's the job, exactly?'

Mr Chipman pointed into the cemetery. 'History. People.'

Jack laughed. 'Good answer.'

'The snow's doing a great service to this place—right now it looks quite picturesque. But let me tell you, underneath that beautiful white blanket are a whole bunch of graves in bad shape. Overgrown, dirty and illegible. Those whose names we *can* read, we know little or nothing about.' He looked earnestly at Jack, his eyes animated and alive. 'These are the people who shaped this town, this county, this state, this country—they deserve better, frankly. Me and some other local history nuts have formed a preservation group and we need someone to help clear and catalogue the cemetery. Someone with a passion for history. And people. Someone willing to go back to school part-time to develop their history knowledge.' He gently tugged his beard. 'Interested?'

Jack smiled. 'Yes. Yes, I am. It sounds perfect—thank you.'

'Excellent,' Mr Chipman said, offering his hand to shake. 'You start on Monday. Come on, let's go defrost ourselves and talk over the finer details with a coffee.'

Jack followed Mr Chipman back out towards the car.

'So what was it you wanted to know about your own family, Jack?' Mr Chipman asked.

'Anything at all,' Jack answered. 'My mom and dad are real cagey about their family. I know that they were both born in Boston, but beyond that is all a bit of a mystery to me. My dad's mom and dad died in an automobile accident in 1946. Dad's two brothers, David and John, were killed in the Second World War. On my mom's side I know that her dad died in the Great Depression and her mom died in 1945. That's it.'

Mr Chipman frowned. 'All a bit tragic, isn't it?'

'Yeah, that's how it sounds,' Jack began, fishing in his back pocket, 'Except, that this morning I found this.' He handed over the certificate. 'I think it's for my dad's marriage—but not to my mom. There are a couple of things wrong with it, including his name, but I think it's him.'

Mr Chipman scanned the certificate as they walked, then stopped in his tracks and gazed at Jack. 'Ah. The witnesses.'

'Exactly. The marriage took place in 1949 and was witnessed by a David Jacklin and George Jacklin. *And* it all took place in California. How could that be?'

Mr Chipman thought for a long while. 'Let me say this to you: does it not strike you as a little unusual that *all* of your mom and dad's family died before...what...1950?'

'Yes—it's always bothered me, but if that's what you're told...'

'Take a step back and view it objectively, Jack. You've been told all this information about your family. But, from one historian to another, I would pose this question: where is the *evidence* to support what you've been told?'

'I don't have any,' Jack admitted.

'All you have so far is that,' he said, pointing to the marriage certificate. He continued to walk back towards the old Saratoga, stepping into the crunchy furrows of their own footprints. 'Now, there may be some explanation—maybe this George and David Jacklin are cousins or other relatives...if not, then it's clear evidence which contradicts the version of events that you've been told. Maybe—and it is just a maybe—the rest of what you know is also untrue.'

Jack's mind was a fog of confusion. Questions rose and fell, vying for him to provide an immediate, sensible answer. His entire understanding of his family's past looked to be completely wrong. He might have uncles, aunts, cousins and grandparents still alive. But why had they lied to him? 'What now?'

Mr Chipman tugged on his beard and answered in a low, thoughtful voice, 'Well, I can look into it for you, if you like? I've got friends who practically live in libraries and Town Halls—both here in Massachusetts and in California—they might be able to turn something up.'

'Yes—yes, please,' Jack replied. Whatever it was, he had resolved to know the truth.

'Okay,' Mr Chipman said, unlocking the car. 'I'll see what I can do. Come on, I'm freezing—let's get out of here.'

They only went to the Dragon Lite Restaurant on special occasions. Tonight's special occasion, the sale of the boxes of junk and war memorabilia, had left Jack with a sharp burning sense of unease. They were sitting close to the window overlooking Main Street, Hyannis, waiting for the food to arrive. Jack decided to make use of his parents' joviality. 'So,' he began, switching his focus between the two of them, 'it's your twenty-third wedding anniversary next month—are you planning on anything special?'

'Is it really?' his dad asked.

'I expect I'll cook your dad's favourite meal, or maybe we'll go out,' his mom said. 'Why do you ask?'

'I just wondered is all. Where did you guys meet, exactly?'

His dad cleared his throat and Jack caught the quick, almost imperceptible flick of his eyes over to his mom. 'Such a long time ago!' he laughed. 'We were just friends when we were young and…'

'Fell in love,' Velda added with a giggle, reaching over and touching her husband's hand.

'But I mean, where were you living?' Jack questioned.

'Boston,' his mom answered.

'And what did your parents think about you getting married?'

Another strange look passed from his dad's eyes.

'They were…' he began.

'Dead before we married,' his mom answered, finishing the sentence.

'Oh yeah, the automobile accident,' Jack said, trying not to sound disingenuous. 'How did that happen, exactly?'

His mom set down her knife and fork and glanced around the restaurant. She leant closer to Jack and lowered her voice. 'Look, what is all this?'

Jack shrugged innocently. 'I'm just curious about my family, is all. I mean, you guys *never* talk about it—' he faced his dad '—I've never even seen a picture of your mom and dad.'

'They're dead,' his mom snapped. 'Now leave it alone.'

'No, it's okay, Velda,' his dad said. 'He has a right to know about what happened. They were out for the evening—I forget where, movie theatre, I think—and there was a real freezing fog hanging over Boston.' He paused to take a breath. He shrugged his shoulders, then continued, 'My mom was driving and she drove right into the back of a truck. The driver—an old veteran—had apparently fallen asleep at the wheel, right in the middle of street and she didn't see him in time. They had no chance. Their car just crumpled up into the back of the truck.'

Jack nodded, unable to look either of them in the eye. It was a damned good story. It might have happened to someone at some point, but *not* to his grandparents in Boston in 1946. He had absolutely no doubt in his mind that they were still alive at the time of his dad's first wedding in 1949.

As far as his mom and dad were concerned, the story had done the trick and had dissolved his curiosity. Their expressions showed that they were poised for further questions. When none came, his dad struck up a conversation about the upcoming election. 'A poll in the paper points to Carter taking the White House.'

And that was that, the discussion switched from a sinking sand of lies to more solid ground, as it always had, he realised.

Jack's expression said that he was listening. In truth, his thoughts were turned firmly to what he had just heard. The words that had been spoken were not in themselves revelatory—indeed, his mom and dad had simply reiterated, with some convincing embellishment, the same narrative that Jack had always known; it was the looks, the body language and the manner of their speech—like they were amateur actors, struggling to recall an exact script from long ago.

The truth was out there, somewhere, and he was going to find it.

Chapter Six

16th August 2016, Barnstable, Massachusetts, USA

Juliette was getting annoyed; Morton could tell that she was biting her tongue and chewing over her choice of words. They were standing in the queue of the Nirvana Coffee Shop on Barnstable Main Street, waiting to order. She drew a long breath—one of her exasperated ones. 'All I'm saying is that you're spending *a lot* of time inspecting the minutiae of your extended family: getting newspaper reports into your grandfather's death, looking at the census for your *great*-grandparents—'

'But I really think that Jack's story is bound up with theirs,' Morton pleaded.

She sighed. 'Look…why are we here?'

Morton glanced around him. 'Coffee.'

'You know full well what I meant—in America—why are we here?'

He thought for a moment, wondering if this was a trick question. 'Honeymoon,' he answered.

'And?'

'To find my father.'

'Precisely!' Juliette asserted. 'To find your *father*—the one thing that you could be doing to help with that, you're avoiding doing.'

She was referring to his Aunt Alice. 'It's not as simple as that.'

Another long breath in. 'It never is with you, is it?'

'What can I get you folks?' the man behind the counter asked.

'Take-out latte for me, please,' Morton ordered, before turning to Juliette. 'Decaf,' he added swiftly for her benefit, despite feeling a desperate need for caffeine right now.

'Same for me,' Juliette said, shaking her head with mock displeasure. 'Look, what is it that you're scared of? That you *don't* find him, or that you *do?*'

It did, in typical Juliette style, cut straight to the heart of the issue. It was, however, only partly true. He was certain that his father's story *was* somehow connected with his grandfather's, but yes, there was a hesitant part of him, content to live forever in ignorance of his father's whereabouts. Right now, his father *could* be alive and delighted at the prospect of meeting his long-lost son. Equally, the opposite could be true; discovering that knowledge was irreversible.

Juliette paid the server and took the two drinks. 'Right,' she said, handing him his latte. 'Today you do whatever it is you're doing. Tomorrow we're exploring Nantucket and Martha's Vineyard, then the next day we're going whale-watching from Provincetown, after which, you're going to find your Aunt Alice. Okay?'

'Fine.'

'See you later,' she said, kissing him on the lips.

'Bye,' he mumbled.

Outside, they headed in opposite directions. He walked briskly, sipping his latte as he went, analysing and regretting their frosty parting. He could tell that at the heart of her contention was the word that she had swallowed down but that had loomed large in the background of their conversation: honeymoon. They were three days into it and had yet to do anything meaningful together. He had spent the entirety of last night researching his family on the internet. His discoveries had taken him well into the early hours of this morning. And now he was feeling it and the decaf wasn't helping matters.

Having found his grandfather's first marriage to Audrey Fuller in 1949, he had discovered the birth of a child, Florence, in 1951. The 1940 census had been revealing. The Jacklin family, all having been born in San Francisco, had an expensive house and a good income from the family hardware business. The next inevitable step had been for him to search for Joseph and Audrey's divorce, which he had found listed in a local newspaper among several other cases to have reached the courts. Joseph Jacklin had filed for divorce in December 1950, citing adultery against his wife, Audrey. The particulars for divorce cases for this period were unfortunately not in the public domain.

Morton went to increase his step, to reach his destination more quickly, when he realised that he had arrived. *Sturgis Library,* the sign announced. *Includes the house built about 1645 by John Lothrop minister of the Barnstable Church from 1639 to 1653.* From the front, the library looked deceptively like a very old house with yellow painted weather-boarding and black-framed windows. The rear of the building, however, incorporated a large extension, to which Morton strode.

Dropping his unfinished drink into a bin outside, he entered the library and walked to the help desk.

'Hi, I'm looking for—'

'The genealogy section?' the young librarian guessed.

'Er, yes, that's right. How did you know?' Morton asked.

'You look like the type,' she said with a smile. 'Follow me.'

'Oh, right.' He didn't know whether looking like a genealogist was a good thing or not.

She led him into a room packed with shelves which were brimming with documents. Hundreds, if not thousands of bound volumes containing Massachusetts vital records. 'What is it you're looking for, exactly?'

Morton grimaced when he paid attention to the dates of the tomes around him: almost all pertained to records ending in the nineteenth century. 'Actually, a bit more recent than this,' he said, before explaining his reasons for coming.

The woman nodded. 'Okay, so through here, then, we have more modern records that might help you.' She took him to the front of the building, in the old house. 'This is the Lothrop Room—built in 1644 for the Reverend John Lothrop, the founder of Barnstable. Lovely, isn't it?'

'Yes, amazing,' Morton agreed, casting his eye around the old room.

'We're the oldest library in the United States and as this very room was used for public worship, so it is also the oldest structure in America where religious services were held.'

'Wow.'

'And it's in here that you'll find voters' lists for the period you're looking for,' she said, pointing to one of the shelves. 'Over here.'

'Thank you very much.'

'Did you say that your dad went to school in this area?'

'I believe so, yes.'

'So, over there we have a collection of the *Barnacle*—the year book from the local high school. When was your dad born?'

'1956,' he answered, watching as the woman's head bobbed around whilst she did a quick mental calculation.

'So, you'll want the 1973 edition,' she said. 'Call me if you need any help with anything.'

'Great—thank you very much,' Morton said, making a beeline for the school year books. Why had he never thought about these before? Perhaps because it was not something usually done in English schools. He selected the one for 1973—a thin silver hardback—and rushed over to the large wooden table in the centre of the room. The first pages were dominated by slightly unflattering photographs of the faculty staff. Next came the section headed *Seniors*.

He paused, holding the page between his fingers. If luck was on his side, he would find a picture of his father in the ensuing pages.

He turned the page and saw the first five students, arranged in alphabetical order. Alongside a headshot photo was a quote from the student, a shortlist of their hobbies and their future goals. Despite wanting to skip through the pages, he took his time. These were his father's classmates—his friends. He looked at the final entry on the page open before him. *Jeanne Elizabeth Hooper*. His father would be on the next page.

With a slow, deliberate movement of his hand, he turned it over. And there he was. His Aunty Margaret had been right. When he had asked her what his father had looked like, her reply had been along the lines of '…take a look at a photo of yourself aged eighteen…' The resemblance was uncanny and irrefutable. Morton knew for certain in that moment, that if he had randomly happened upon this photograph he would have known categorically that it was his father. Only his hair—styled in an elaborate wave—set him in the seventies. He looked at the picture for a long time.

Finally, he allowed his eyes to move from the photo to the caption below it. His classmates' quotes had been poetic, inspirational, motivating. '*Yesterday's hurt is today's understanding rewoven into tomorrow's love.*' '*If at first you don't succeed, don't worry about it, you'll get another chance.*' '*He who gives love, gets love.*'

Morton grinned as he read his father's entry. He clearly had a sense of humour. *Keep smiling. It makes people wonder what you've been up to.* Then he read his father's hobbies and future plans. *Enjoys music, history, milkshakes…plans travel and college.* Evidently being blamed for his father's death in a house fire three years later, then disappearing from the face of the earth hadn't figured into his plans in 1973. Neither had having a child just a year later.

Morton couldn't take his eyes off the photograph and mini-biography. Solid genealogical evidence that this man existed. His father. He was getting closer to finding him.

Having taken a series of photographs of the page, Morton pushed on through the book. He found his father in another photo—a group shot of the student council. It was more formal and official in appearance—taken on the school stage by the look of it, with around twenty students facing the camera with their hands together in front of them.

His father turned up again, twice more. Once standing fully kitted up with three other members of the hockey club and once in a list of *Perfect Barnstable High School Boy and Girl*, winning best smile.

The yearbook painted a happy picture for his father's time at school.

Despite feeling like he needed to get on, Morton returned to the front of the book and photographed every single page. Besides his father's birth certificate, it was the only tangible thing that Morton had that made his father a real person, and not simply a name plucked from history.

Having photographed the year book, Morton carried it back to the shelf. He held it in his hands for a moment longer, before placing it back. Then, he turned to the rows of voters' lists, pulling 1976 from the shelf and placing it on the table. *Town of Barnstable. List of persons seventeen years of age or over. Listed as residents thereof by the Registrars of Voters on January 1, 1976.*

The streets were listed in alphabetical order. Morton flipped straight to Ocean Avenue and ran his finger down the page until he reached number 256.

Chipman, Bertram J.　　**Retired**
Chipman, Michael H.　　**Student**
Chipman, Laura J.　　**Student**

Morton photographed the entry, evaluating the information. The most likely scenario was that his father had gone to the house because of Michael Chipman. In his final letter to Margaret in December 1976, Jack had written that he was staying with a friend who was 'lending him everything.' Morton guessed that Laura was Michael's sister and Bertram was their father.

'School friends?' Morton questioned to himself, leaping up and grabbing the 1973 high school yearbook again. Flipping just a few pages inside, he found Michael Chipman. And Laura. Twins.

As he looked at their headshots, Morton was certain that they held the key to locating his father. His next steps would be to try and track them down.

Opening his laptop, he ran an online search in the White Pages. Three hundred and eighty-nine Chipmans currently living in Massachusetts. He narrowed the search for Michael. One result. But it was the wrong middle initial and wrong age bracket. Searches for Laura and Bertram also proved to be unsuccessful.

Returning to the voters' lists, Morton found the family had continued to reside in Ocean Avenue until 1982, when another family had moved in.

Switching between various genealogy websites, Morton ran a series of searches into the Chipmans. His naïve hope that perhaps one of them still lived in the area abruptly disappeared. There was no sign of Laura in official records. The Social Security Index at Ancestry informed him that Bertram Chipman had died in 1982 and Michael had died in 2007.

Morton closed his laptop and packed up to leave the library.

He was fast running out of options.

Chapter Seven

4th August 1950, Cow Hollow, San Francisco, California, USA

It was lunchtime and, despite the chill in the air, the clear skies and high sun had lured people to the open green expanses and panoramic views of the city and sea that were offered by the Fort Mason recreation area. Picnic blankets and park benches were adorned with a motley collection of workers on late lunches, mothers with young children, students, lovers and vagrants.

Velda Henderson ambled along a path that wound its way steeply up from the Aquatic Park Pier. She took a cursory glance to her right to the Golden Gate Bridge. The iconic structure that pulled thousands of visitors to the city each year held over her a constant dark allure. Her mother had succumbed to it and Velda had, on two separate occasions, almost yielded to it, too.

She shuddered, loathing the power that a simple steel structure seemed to hold over her life.

The path finally levelled out and Velda paused to catch her breath. She wanted to sit down—find a bench and eat her sandwich. The first benches at the top of the path were taken, so she continued walking.

She stopped again, this time not to regain her breath, but to avoid being seen. She leapt to the side and ducked down, much to the bemusement of the three occupants—businessmen—sitting on the bench nearest her.

She slowly stood up to check if what she had seen had been correct. It was—Audrey canoodling with another man. So, the rumours that she had been fornicating with someone from her office had been true. And not just any other man, but Dwight Kalinski—the CEO, who was supposedly a devout Catholic, married with four children.

Velda watched incredulously. Audrey had her skirt hitched up higher than was decent and Dwight was running his hand along the length of her thigh. It was just typical of Audrey Fuller—Velda couldn't bring herself to use her married surname—she craved the unobtainable. The trouble was, her confidence matched her looks in equal measure and most times she got what she wanted. And when she got it, she lost all interest and moved onto some*thing* or some*one* else. It had always been the same—at school, with jobs, with men; if she couldn't have it, she wanted it all the more.

Poor Joseph. She would have to tell him. Perhaps this time he might listen. Especially since her last warning had proven to be correct; Audrey hadn't been pregnant at all.

But could she tell him now, *really*? He was out—God only knows where, somewhere in Korea—fighting for his country. Was it really acceptable to burden him with such devastating news, just five months after their wedding day? Yes, she quickly decided, it was her duty. She had heard from Joseph's brother that the early months of the marriage had been turbulent and that on several occasions their fighting had led to Joseph returning to his old bedroom in his parents' house.

Velda took one last look, just to be certain, just to rule out any doubt that they were just being friendly. She slowly extended herself onto tiptoes and looked over at the bench. She needn't have been so cautious—Audrey and Dwight were in the throes of a lengthy and passionate kiss—she could have been sitting beside them and they would have been none the wiser.

Velda ran back the way that she had come—faster than she could remember ever running before in her life—all the way home.

She didn't want to waste a single second in writing a letter to Joseph. *Her* Joseph.

Chapter Eight

15th March 1976, Lothrop Hill Cemetery, Barnstable, Massachusetts, USA

Jack was out of breath. He slumped down with his back to the gnarled trunk of an eastern white pine and drank the last mouthful of water from his bottle. His work was done for the day. All around him were great ugly pyres of giant hogweed roots and a host of other pernicious weeds which had consumed the cemetery. From the cleared scrubland had emerged gravestones with hand-chiselled names which had not seen the light of day for several years. *Hinkley. Strugis. Chipman. Lothrop.* The early settlers who had helped create and shape the town and county.

Jack was pleased with his achievements. He and he alone had now cleared three quarters of the cemetery. Mr Chipman would pop by every so often and praise his efforts, usually delighting in some freshly uncovered headstone, but it had been he who had been responsible for returning some semblance of life to the place.

He watched as a cardinal glided down from the tree above him, landing on a nearby headstone. Jack watched the bright red bird, embracing the peace and satisfaction which he had craved whilst working at Rory's Store. There really was no comparison between the two jobs.

The cardinal flew away with a chipping cry.

'What's this—slacking on the job?'

Jack laughed, raising his hand to shield his eyes from the sun that loomed directly behind Mr Chipman's head.

'You've done well, Jack,' he praised. 'Good job. Now time to pack up for the weekend.'

'Thanks, I'm done in—ready for a nice hot bath,' Jack replied, standing and stretching. He began to gather up his tools.

'I'll get these piles burnt tomorrow then there's not much more to do before you start phase two.'

'I can't wait,' Jack said. Phase two was to clean and transcribe each and every headstone. Phase three, which he was looking forward to most of all, was to trawl the town and state archives, searching out information on these founding settlers.

'Here you go,' Mr Chipman said, fishing in his trouser pockets. 'Your wages for the week.' He handed Jack a bunch of notes.

'Thank you,' Jack said, removing a twenty-dollar bill and passing it back over to Mr Chipman. 'For the box.'

It took a second for Mr Chipman to register and reach out for the money. 'Oh, yeah, the box.'

When Jack had lamented to Mr Chipman that his dad had sold a box of old family memorabilia, he had driven Jack directly to the antique store and purchased them back again for three hundred dollars. The box was now in storage in Mr Chipman's garage and Jack was paying him back weekly.

'Jack,' Mr Chipman began, fiddling with the tip of his beard.

'Yes?'

'I've had an initial report back, you know, into what I said I would find out for you. I'm afraid there's no record anywhere of your family in Boston.'

Jack nodded, his expectations confirmed.

'Your parents only appear on voter lists for Cape Cod from 1953 onwards.'

'Really?' Jack questioned. 'You're sure?'

Mr Chipman nodded. 'And another thing: your dad's two brothers. One of them—John—*was* killed in the war but the other one—David—was *not*.'

'I don't understand...'

'My acquaintances are still looking into it for you...but these things take time—it's not easy.'

'I know—and I really do appreciate your helping me. So one of my uncles is still alive?'

'Well, I didn't say that. I said that he didn't die in the Second World War—there's a difference.'

'But he might be alive.'

'Maybe.' Mr Chipman reached out and touched Jack's arm. 'Jack, may I ask you a question?'

'Sure—go ahead.'

'How is it that your parents live where they do? I mean, they're neighbors with the Kennedys and yet your father runs a car lot.'

The question—so obvious, yet one that he had never considered in depth before—threw him. His parents had certainly never been ones to splash money around and yet, yes, they did live in one of the nicest areas on Cape Cod. 'I don't know.' Jack looked blankly to Mr Chipman. Clearly *he* had some idea.

'I don't know either, it's just something that has always puzzled me, but it's been none of my business to ask. I always *assumed* there was some inherited wealth involved, which is why I do feel it's appropriate to ask now. Maybe there's a connection to your father's past life?'

'Maybe,' Jack said absentmindedly. The way that Mr Chipman had said *'past life'* sent a chill through Jack's bones. The implication was clear: his father had not simply relocated from one part of the country to another; he had existed as a different person in a different place. Jack saw it now as a kind of reincarnation of sorts. And the evidence was growing.

Jack entered the house, kicked off his boots and hung up his coat. 'Hello?' he yelled, although he knew from the absence of their cars on the front drive that his parents were not yet home. 'Hello? Mom? Dad?' he called, moving slowly along the hallway.

The house replied with silence.

The hallway clock told him that they were due back at any moment.

The place was empty, yet still he trod lightly, as though he were creeping over a frozen lake. He reached his dad's study—tucked away at the end of the hallway beside the laundry room. The door was always kept shut and visitors were not readily admitted.

Jack opened the door and stepped inside. A couple of years ago, he and Alice had speculated at the secretive nature of the room. Their joking about their dad being a Russian spy, serial killer or Mafioso boss resulted, one day, when they were alone together in the house, in them goading each other into entering the room. Their childish opening of cupboards, looking for bodies, guns or a stash of money had of course resulted in nothing remotely interesting. All they had found were books and files containing home and business finances. They had left the room giggling that their dad was *definitely* a Russian serial-killing Mafia warlord.

If Jack remembered correctly, he had seen files containing bank statements behind his dad's grand mahogany desk. He hurried over to the shelf and scanned along the handwritten labels until he found 'Personal Banking June 30, 1974 - July 1, 1975' on the edge of a box file. He took it down and began to rummage inside. As he had expected, the filing was meticulous. Jack removed the most recent bank statement in the box and ran his finger down the outgoings column.

He didn't have time to scrutinise each and every transaction, but there were no figures that struck him as abnormal. Switching his focus to the income column, he spotted it immediately. Two amounts came in that month: $400 and $5000. Jack traced his finger along the page to the source of the money—both were from two separate numbered accounts.

He guessed that the lower amount was for his dad's wages. From where, then, did the higher—significantly higher—amount come?

Flicking through to the previous month, he found exactly the same two figures coming in. The same for the month before that.

Jack placed the file back on the shelf and pulled down the next one. He opened the box, then froze. He thought that he heard the sound of a car door slamming. He quickly returned the box to the shelf, hurried towards the door and peered out. Through the two narrow panes of glass in the door, Jack could see his dad, reaching up to place his key in the lock. There was no way he could get clear of this end of the hallway.

Jack rushed out of the study, pushed the door closed behind him and darted into the adjacent laundry room, tossed his t-shirt into the wash basket and then walked slowly out into the hallway.

'Oh, hi,' Jack greeted his dad.

His dad nodded, a note of suspicion in his cocked eyebrow. He stood as motionless as a mannequin, his hand frozen to his fedora hat, as he regarded Jack. 'Hi.'

'Just putting my shirt in the laundry,' Jack said by way of explanation, as he took the stairs two at a time, grimacing as he went, hoping that he hadn't aroused his dad's suspicions.

He closed his bedroom door and threw himself onto the bed, knitting his fingers together behind his head. God, he hoped that he had put the files back correctly. His dad would certainly spot it if they were even half an inch out of place. Fiercely guarding his *past life*. Jack had absolutely no clue what was going on. Was it really such a big deal that he had been married before? Not to Jack, no. Divorce was just a normal part of life, nowadays. *Maybe it wasn't so common back then*, he thought. Maybe embarrassment or shame had bred secrets which had perpetuated, lingered and slowly morphed into lies which had grown larger with each passing year. Was that it? But then why pretend that all your family is dead? He wished he had someone with whom to talk it over. He had Mr Chipman, of course, but he wasn't really someone in whom Jack felt he could confide. If only Laura and Michael were still around. Or Alice. Yes, she would be good to discuss it with. Perhaps he could take a trip down to Boston sometime and see her.

It was strange because after Laura, Michael and Alice, the next person with whom Jack felt he wanted to talk was Margaret. He'd only known her for a week and here he was wanting to spill all of his family secrets to her. He guessed that meant that they'd had a connection.

Reaching into his bedside table, Jack took out some paper and a pen. *Dear Margaret, I really hope you're doing well. I know you won't reply to my letters—maybe you're not even getting them—but, in a way, that helps. You're my silent friend! Life here is getting real strained. Since the vacation to England I've found out some stuff about my dad—not good stuff! I don't really want to write it down, just in case… Let's just say it's from his past and that it isn't great—even Mom doesn't know about it.*

'Jack!' his dad shouted from downstairs. 'Jack!'

Jack quickly tucked the unfinished letter into his bedside table and opened his bedroom door. 'Yeah?' he called down, hoping that the wavering of guilt in that single word was indiscernible to his dad.

'I'm running down to the store—do you want to come? Or do you need anything?'

'No, I'm good, thanks. I'm just going to take a bath.'

'Okay, I'll be right back.'

Jack stood rigid, clutching the door, breathing lightly until he heard the roar of his dad's car outside. Seconds later, the sound faded to nothing. Jack darted from his room, down the stairs and back along to his dad's study, where his trembling fingers fumbled back through the paperwork that he had just seen.

Picking up the phone, Jack dialled a number.

The delay before the call was answered was short yet interminable.

'Hello, Cape Cod Five Cents Savings Bank, this is Susie, how may I help you today?'

'Good afternoon, this is Mr Jacklin,' Jack said, before relaying his dad's account number.

'What can I do for you today, Mr Jacklin?'

'Could I give you the details of an account that credits me every month, please?'

'Sure, go ahead.'

Jack told her the details then asked, 'Is it possible to have the date that the credit transaction occurs changed at all?'

'Well, that's not something we can do this end, I'm afraid. You'd need to contact the Union Bank in San Francisco and request that they change the date for you—it shouldn't be a problem.'

'Okay, that's great—thank you so much.'

'Will that be everything, Mr Jacklin?'

'Yes, thank you. Goodbye.'

Jack ended the call, returned the file to the shelf and quietly slipped towards the door. He pulled it open and gasped.

'Hello, Jack,' his mom said.

Chapter Nine

18th August 2016, off the coast of Provincetown, Massachusetts, USA

God only knew how his mobile had found a signal. It was patchy enough around his hometown in Rye, and yet here, in the middle of the Atlantic Ocean, with not an inch of land to be seen in any direction, his mobile had found sufficient signal to push through his emails. One email to be precise, from Keith Grant of *Grant Funeral Home*.

'Oh wow! Did you see that one?' Juliette extolled, her voice unified with dozens of others aboard *The Dolphin IX*, all out for a three-hour whale-watching experience.

They were pressed to a white railing on the side of the boat. Morton looked up from his mobile to see a shattered disc of water tumbling back into the sea, presumably in the wake of a humpback.

'You didn't see it, did you?' Juliette asked accusingly.

'Yes, I saw it. It was a whale,' Morton said flatly.

'What are you doing?' she quizzed.

'Reading an email from *Grant Funeral Home*.'

'What did they say?'

'*Dear Morton, Thank you for your email. I can confirm that we handled your grandfather's funeral. It took place on 8th January 1977. He was buried in a two-person plot in Old Neck Cemetery, Hyannis. Our records show that he was born April 3rd, 1928 in Boston, MA and died December 24th, 1976 in Hyannis Port, MA. No further interments have taken place in this plot and the grave is registered to the deceased's widow, Velda Jacklin. Her address has changed several times over the years, the most recent we have dates to 2012 and is for White Oaks Care Home, Hyannis. I hope this information has been of use to you. Yours, K. Grant.*'

'Does that mean your grandmother's still alive?' Juliette asked.

'It means she *was* alive four years ago. Maybe she still is, maybe not. She hasn't been buried with her husband and she'd be eighty-seven, so it's not unreasonable to assume she's still alive.'

Juliette's eyes narrowed as she met his gaze. 'Gosh, you might actually get to meet your grandmother. How exciting. Shall we try and visit her after this?'

Morton nodded and looked out over the bow of the boat. Land was looming. He spotted the two-hundred-and-fifty-feet-tall Pilgrim Monument which towered over their destination, Provincetown and began to feel the pang of anxiety which had gripped him upon arrival. Without looking for it, they had found his aunt's place of work. *Alice's Art* was a small wooden hut on MacMillan Pier—just yards from their point of departure for whale-watching. It had been with some relief that they had found the hut closed. 'She obviously likes a lie-in,' Juliette had quipped, looking at the opening times on the door. 'It'll be open by the time we return.'

'Great,' Morton had said half-heartedly. Of course he wanted to see her—he *needed* to see her, but he genuinely feared the outcome of their meeting.

As they powered on towards the shore, more and more of the town drew into focus. The long blurred line of beachfront property began to detach into distinct houses, hotels and businesses. Sun revellers and bathers enjoying the hot sands surrounding the town on all sides pulled into sharpness.

From behind a large grey fisherman's building appeared Macmillan Pier. Juliette took his hand in hers and gave it a long squeeze. He knew that she had seen it, too: *Alice's Art* was open. There was no turning back now—they *had* to walk past it, like it or not.

The boat slowed down to a gentle crawl—taking away the welcome breeze that had offset the airless heat of the day—nudging close to the pier moorings. A general agitation rippled around them, as the passengers began to gather their belongings and move towards the exit at the rear of the boat.

'Let's let everyone else off first,' Morton said, taking a seat for the first time on the voyage. He sat with a noisy sigh that reminded him of his late adoptive father. Without fail, every time he had sat down—or stood up again, for that matter—he would emit a guttural grunt which, at the time, used to annoy Morton. The memory of it now made him smile. He wondered how he would have broached this transatlantic search for his biological father with him. Their already strained relationship had worsened after Morton had inadvertently revealed his desire to find his father. He had died not long after.

'Come on, then,' Juliette urged, tugging at his left arm.

Morton looked around him. Apart from a final few stragglers, the boat had emptied out onto the pier. He stood up and walked together with Juliette off the boat.

It was hot and swarming with tourists milling in and out of the various huts that adorned the pier, like bees around a run of hives. *Alice's Art* was right in the centre of the row.

Morton gripped Juliette's hand. His nerves were beginning to rattle inside him, making his breathing and walking more laboured than usual.

'Just breathe deeply,' Juliette reassured him. 'I'll be there with you.'

They reached the hut. Morton quickly scanned the people standing nearby. Nobody here who looked like Alice's profile picture on Facebook.

'Shall we go inside?' Juliette asked.

'I just want to look at these,' he said, pointing to a display of flora and fauna painted onto what looked like driftwood. 'Do you like it?'

Juliette shrugged. 'It's okay—as procrastination devices go.'

'I like it,' Morton said, ignoring her provocation.

'It's a northern cardinal painted onto snow fence wood,' a female voice explained.

Morton froze momentarily.

'We get some pretty fierce winters out here and, when the fences are done, we get given them.'

'It's lovely,' Morton said, turning to face her.

'Yeah, we…' The look between them snapped the end of whatever she had been about to say.

He knew that it was her the moment that she had first opened her mouth; her appearance only served as a confirmation. She looked just like her pictures on the internet—unruly curly hair, dark eyes and exotically coloured hessian clothes. 'It's forty dollars,' she said, a dour indignation blighting her face and words. 'I'll be inside if you want to make a purchase.' She whirled around and disappeared inside the hut.

'Why didn't you introduce yourself?' Juliette asked.

'I didn't need to…She knew,' Morton replied.

'Go in after her, then!'

He had to. Even though it wasn't going to go well, he had to try at least. He set down the piece of art and marched inside the hut. It was filled with an assortment of paintings, coasters, mugs and sculptures featuring Cape Cod life and wildlife.

'Can we talk, please?' Morton asked, touching Alice's arm.

She flinched, pulling her arm back sharply, as though he had just prodded her with a hot poker. 'I'm *working*.'

'Can we meet, then? I've come all the way from England to—'

'Then I'm afraid you've had a wasted trip,' she seethed. 'I've nothing to say to you.'

Morton was stunned. Wounded. Where could he go from that?

'Can I help you, sir?' a lady asked from behind him. She wore an apron that might once have been white but was now daubed with the smudges from more hues of paint than Morton knew existed. She was a middle-aged lady with short white hair. She smiled. 'Is everything okay, Alice?'

'This gentleman is from England—he's just leaving.'

'Oh…right…I see.'

Morton turned back to face Alice. 'Here's my card,' he said quietly, setting down one of his business cards, before turning to leave. He found Juliette outside, her face one of sympathy. She took his hand in hers.

'I can't believe she could be like that—she's your flesh and blood, for goodness' sake. I really thought that once we got here and you—'

'I don't want to talk about it. Let's go and get a coffee—large and very caffeinated.'

Macmillan Pier ran directly to the centre of Provincetown's Commercial Street. The narrow road was lined with an assortment of galleries, guesthouses, gift shops, cafés and restaurants, all heaving with the great influx of summer holidaymakers that had reawakened the town from its winter slumber.

They walked silently, taking in the sights around them as they went.

'Do you want to go in here?' Juliette asked of several shops around which he might ordinarily have enjoyed browsing. But not now; his mind simply wasn't on anything other than how to find his father in the time that he had left in Massachusetts. Michael Chipman was dead. His Aunt Alice might as well have been. Everything now rested on his eighty-seven-year-old grandmother. Could he really just rock up to her care home and introduce himself? Was that acceptable or appropriate?

'Right, we're going in here,' Juliette instructed, dragging him off the pavement and onto the outside area of Joe's Coffee and Café. 'You sit down and get your laptop open and I'll get the drinks. Iced coffee?'

'*Coffee* coffee,' he stated, slinking obediently down at a table for two. He removed his laptop from his bag and opened it up, although he wasn't sure what he was actually going to do now that it was up and running, so he just sat there people-watching until Juliette returned.

She placed the drinks on the table. 'One *coffee* coffee,' she announced, pulling her chair so that it was beside his. 'Where are we up to?'

'What do you mean?'

'What's the next step? You're a forensic genealogist—you've always got a next step. Obviously we're going to try and visit your grandmother this afternoon. What else have you got to work on?'

Morton sighed. 'I could try and work on my grandfather's brothers in San Francisco—maybe try and trace their descendants, see if they know what happened to my father.'

Juliette turned her nose up. 'Anything closer to home? Pass me your folder.'

Morton obliged and took a sip of the coffee.

Juliette began to scrutinise each document in her typical police officer manner. 'What's this?' 'Have you thought about trying to…' 'What does this mean?' Finally, she set the paperwork down, took a mouthful of her drink then turned to him, like a judge summarising a case in her court. 'So, your grandfather and grandmother stick to this party line, that he was born and raised in Boston, despite both knowing this to be untrue. They married in Wellfleet in 1953 and then settled in Hyannis Port, where your father and Aunt Alice were born. Your grandfather, though, actually grew up in San Francisco, where he married Audrey…remind me of her surname?'

'Fuller.'

'Audrey Fuller. They married in 1949. His divorce was mentioned in the papers in…?'

'December 1950.'

'I take it there's no US census for 1950?'

Morton shook his head. 'Not available until 2022.'

'Hang on a minute,' Juliette said, rummaging back in the folder. 'This,' she said, wafting his grandfather's death certificate in front of his face, 'says that he served in the Korean War. Wasn't that in the early fifties? Or am I getting my dates mixed up?'

'1950 to 1953,' Morton confirmed. He realised, as though a switch had been illuminated in his mind, where she was going with this line of thought. 'How was he around to divorce his wife *and* fight on a different continent?'

'It's worth pursuing. Maybe you were right—maybe your father's disappearance does have connections to this anomaly in your grandfather's past. Who knows? Other than that—could you put an advert in the local paper? See if anyone else your father went to school with is still around and knows his whereabouts? He can't have only been friends with the Chipman family, after all.'

'Both are very good ideas,' he agreed.

'I know,' she laughed, sitting back and drinking her drink. 'Us genealogy widows have our uses, you know.'

Morton smiled as he began to investigate records pertaining to the Korea War. Owing to privacy restrictions, few service records for the period were in the public domain. He started by typing the name Roscoe Jacklin into the search page of Fold3, a genealogy website specialising in military records. Unsurprisingly, the search returned zero results. When he changed the Christian name to Joseph, there was one result. He clicked the entry. It was found in the *Medal of Honor Roll.*

'Listen to this,' Morton said. 'Rank and Organisation: *Sergeant First Class, U.S. Army, 2nd Reconnaissance Company, 2nd Infantry Division.* Place and date: *Near Yongsan, Korea, November 1st 1950.* Birth: *San Francisco, California.* Citation: *Jacklin distinguished himself by conspicuous gallantry and intrepidity above and beyond the call of duty in action against the enemy. While participating in an assault to secure a key terrain feature, Jacklin's squad was pinned down by withering small arms, mortar and machinegun fire. Although already wounded, he left the comparative safety of his position and made a daring charge against the machinegun emplacement. Within ten yards of the goal, he was again wounded by small arms fire but continued on, entered the bunker, killed two hostile soldiers with his rifle, a third with his bayonet, and silenced the machinegun. Inspired by this incredible display of bravery, the men hastily moved up and completed their mission, and more than 100 hostile troops abandoned their weapons and fled in disorganized retreat. Jacklin, exhausted and injured, then became detached from the division for several days. Jacklin's indomitable courage, extraordinary heroism, and superb leadership reflect the highest credit on himself and are in keeping with the esteemed traditions of the infantry and the U.S. Army.*'

'Wow. I'm not sure if he was extraordinarily heroic or extraordinarily stupid, but wow—that's your grandfather,' Juliette commented.

Morton looked again at the entry. 'So this happened on the first of November 1950. I'm guessing that he was then discharged from the army and repatriated.'

'One month later he files for divorce,' Juliette added.

'Three years later, he's three thousand miles away with a new wife, new past and a new name.'

'Is it reading too much between the lines to suggest that the incident in Korea changed him?' Juliette pondered. 'You know, he came back a different man, didn't want Audrey anymore, but his childhood sweetheart from next door—that sort of thing?'

Morton thought for a moment. The same idea had occurred to him but there was little genealogical fact with which to support it.

'What happened to the daughter from the first marriage? Any trace of her?'

Morton shook his head. 'She doesn't show up in the Social Security Index and I can't find a marriage for her, but that doesn't mean she *didn't* marry.'

'Another mystery,' Juliette laughed.

'Hmm,' Morton agreed. Ordinarily, he loved the challenge of trying to unravel a complex and seemingly unsolvable genealogical mystery—it was something upon which he had built his career—but just for once he wished for a simple, straightforward case.

He quickly wrote an email to the *Cape Cod Times*, requesting that they print an appeal for information on his father, then closed his laptop and sat back to enjoy a coffee with his wife in the glorious Provincetown sunshine.

'Well, here we are,' Morton said, tucking the hire car into a bay in front of the White Oaks care home. He switched off the engine and looked up at the building. Cladded in a juxtaposition of oak panelling and off-white render, it looked modern, purpose-built. It was an amazingly odd feeling to think that his grandmother—a lady on whom he had never clapped his eyes—had a room somewhere inside those walls. Or at least did have up to four years ago.

'Come on, let's get inside—I need some air-con,' Juliette said, leading the way to the main entrance. The automatic doors slid open and they found themselves in a reception that was more like a hotel lobby than a care home. It was spacious, open and, best of all, cool. Morton approached the front desk, unsure of exactly how he was going to explain himself.

'Hi. Can I help you?' a chirpy lady in a white coat said from behind the desk.

'Hello,' Morton began. 'I've come over from England to see my grandmother—she's a resident here.' He figured that a simple get-to-the-point statement was much better than the elaborate alternative.

The lady smiled. 'How lovely. And what's your grandmother's name?'

'Velda. Velda Jacklin.'

Another smile. 'Lovely Velda,' she said, tapping something into the computer in front of her.

She was alive, then, surely?

'And what's your name, please?'

'Morton Farrier.'

More tapping. Then a frown. 'I'm afraid you're not listed here as family. There are no grandchildren listed. Morton, you say?'

Now the story began to get complicated. 'She doesn't know about me, I'm her son's son.'

'She doesn't have any sons listed, either.' She looked up at him. 'I'm very sorry, sir, but I can't let you see her.'

'But I'm her grandson,' Morton protested.

'But you must understand, sir, we can't just let anyone in who claims to be related; our residents are very vulnerable with a whole range of healthcare needs.'

'I do understand, but I've come a very long way to see her.'

She sighed. 'Do you have any documentation that shows you're related to her?'

There was a question. 'No, I don't.'

She shrugged. 'There's nothing I can do, sir, I'm sorry—I really am.'

'Can I speak to a manager, please?' Morton pressed, becoming more agitated as the chances of him meeting his grandmother were slipping away before his eyes.

The lady didn't answer, but picked up the phone. 'Diane, could you come down here, please? I've got someone who wants to speak with you. Thank you.'

'Thanks,' Morton murmured, ambling away from the desk.

Moments later a lady in her early sixties, with a tight black perm and pristine white coat, appeared. She leant over the desk and a brief, hushed conversation took place between the receptionist and her, then she walked over to Morton with her hand extended. 'Hi there, I'm Diane. I understand your grandmother is a resident here, but you don't have any documentation to prove that you're related to her?'

'Yes, that's right. Do you have five minutes for me to explain?' Morton asked.

'Sure, come right this way.' Diane led Juliette and him around to an office behind the reception desk. 'Take a seat.'

'Right,' Morton began. 'Where to start...'

It took him ten minutes of uninterrupted explanation to get to a point where he felt he could draw breath and sit back, his case delivered. He interspersed his monologue by showing her some of the documents that related to his search, in the hope that it lent him some degree of credibility.

For the most part, Diane had remained expressionless. Now that he was finished, she clasped her hands together on the desk and leant in. 'Okay. I'm sure you appreciate that I can't just let anyone in to see our residents. *Some* of our residents have been here for a long time. *Some* of them have severe dementia and wouldn't be able to engage in a rational conversation. Okay?'

Morton understood.

Diane paused. 'I can't allow anyone to walk in off the streets with no clear paperwork…'

Morton nodded, accepting that his quest was over. 'Okay,' he said, standing. 'Thank you for your time.'

'But…' Diane continued. 'We *do* allow volunteers in to sit for just a few minutes and have *general* conversations with our residents.' She cocked her head to one side and opened her hands out. 'It helps them.'

Morton smiled. 'My wife Juliette and I would very much like to volunteer to come and chat with your residents,' he said seriously.

Diane smiled. 'Of course, that would be real nice. I'll just go and get you some badges and get you signed in, then I'll take you to the lounge.' Diane left the room.

Morton turned to Juliette with a grin.

'So she's got dementia—tread very carefully, Morton or you'll get thrown out,' Juliette whispered.

'I will.'

Diane returned with a form to complete and two badges. 'If you fill these in, I'll take you through.'

Having completed the forms and pinned on their badges, Morton and Juliette followed Diane in through a security-coded door, along a long warm corridor with glass walls overlooking two spacious lounges.

Diane stopped at the end of the corridor. 'That lounge over there is for residents who have some degree of independence—they come and go as they please to their rooms. This side' —she indicated to the room beside them— 'this is where residents with more complex needs come. I suggest we go in here.' She tapped another keypad then pushed open the door.

Morton gazed around the room. He reckoned that there were around twenty elderly residents dotted about on chairs that could cater for double that number. A handful of carers were doing a variety of jobs around the room.

Diane turned to face them and spoke in a low voice. 'Okay, when you speak to someone with dementia, you need to speak in short, simple sentences. Speak more slowly than usual and avoid asking too many questions. The two ladies I'm going to take you to often get confused and say things that don't make any sense. Obviously don't raise your voice and avoid speaking about them as if they weren't there. If they say things that you know are not true, don't contradict them, but just keep quiet. Okay?'

'Fine,' Morton agreed.

'Let's go over and see these two lovely ladies, here,' Diane said loudly. She led them over to two elderly women and crouched down in front of them. 'Ladies, we've got some volunteers in to come and chat with you for a few minutes. This is Juliette and this is Morton. Juliette, this is Clarissa; Morton, this… is Velda.'

Juliette sat next to Clarissa and instantly struck up a conversation of sorts.

Morton smiled and waved awkwardly, then sat beside Velda. From nowhere, his eyes glistened with moisture as he took her in. His grandmother. She had a lined, round face and short, style-less white hair. He studied her features, wanting to absorb every detail, knowing that it would likely be the one and only time that he would ever see her. Her grey eyes held something that resembled acute grief to Morton, as though they were sheltering some great loss inside.

He wiped his eyes and finally spoke. 'Hello, Velda.'

'Hello,' she responded, eyeing him up and down. 'I expect you've come to fix the vacuum, have you? I told the store it was broken…oh, sometime last week. I'm sure it's the thing—you know—the motor? That's always the problem. Always.'

'Yes, I think you're right,' Morton said quietly.

'Alice will be here soon,' Velda said. 'You remember her, don't you?'

'I know her, yes,' Morton answered.

'Of course you do. She used to look after me. You don't come see me.'

'I'd like to see you more often, but I live in England.'

Velda sat up straight and looked at her friend beside her. 'Did you hear that? He lives in England now. We didn't know where he went. Now he fixes vacuums.' She waved her hand towards Diane. 'Hey, Missy—did you feed the…the…'

'Dog?' Diane said. 'Yes, Velda, I fed the dog.'

Velda shook her head. 'Always the way. Always.' She turned back to Morton. 'She's twenty-three—doesn't look it, but she is.'

'She's a lovely person. Very kind,' Morton said, receiving a warm smile back from Diane.

'Who is? The cook?' Velda laughed. 'You should try his meatballs—urgh! Every day I have them for breakfast with some other…I don't know. Just awful.' She pushed closer to Morton and scrunched up her face. 'You're new—I haven't seen you before. What do you want?'

'I came to see you,' Morton said softly.

'Hmm, I bet you did. Not a bad place I've got here, is it?' Velda gazed happily around the room. 'Real nice—we bought it…I don't know…Hey! Missy, when did we buy this place?'

Diane made the pretence of thinking for a moment then shook her head. 'A long time ago.'

Velda agreed. 'Yeah, a long time ago. It's got a television!'

'Really? What do you like to watch?' Morton asked.

Velda blew out a puff of air but said nothing.

'Do you want me to take your photo, Morton?' Diane asked.

'Yes, that would be lovely—thank you.' He handed her his mobile.

'Smile!' Diane chirped.

'I knew you'd come back for me, Jack,' Velda said. 'I'm sorry for what I did.'

She thought he was Jack. 'That's okay,' Morton said. He felt like he'd been kicked in the stomach. He looked at Diane, then at Juliette, desperate to ask further questions in the guise of his father. But he just couldn't do it.

'Can you get those cars switched off?' Velda barked at Diane. She turned to Morton with an apologetic shake of her head. 'I keep asking…can I *have* a hot chocolate?'

'I'll rustle you one up shortly,' Diane said. 'Just you keep on chatting to your visitor—he's come from England.'

'England?' Velda exclaimed. 'I went there once.' She looked at Morton then laughed. 'With you! And now you've got a car vacuum or something?' She sagged down in her seat. 'Always the same. When's my mother getting here? She's late again. She would love England. Do you remember Buckingham Palace?'

'Yes, I do—you're allowed inside now,' Morton said.

'Who is? The cook or my mother? They're both dead.' Velda laughed exaggeratedly, then wiped her nose on the back of her hand.

'I'm about ready for bed. Missy, get rid of this man—I don't want to talk about vacuums.'

Diane stood up. 'Okay, I think it's probably time to let these ladies have a rest now.'

'Yes,' Morton said, standing up. He leant down and touched Velda's hand. He knew it was probably forbidden, but he didn't care. 'Goodbye, Velda. It was really lovely to meet you.'

Velda withdrew her hand, a look of disgust on her face. She grunted something and turned away, muttering her displeasure to her friend.

He and Juliette followed Diane from the lounge back out into the corridor. Morton watched Velda through the glass walls until she was out of sight.

'Thank you so much for that,' Morton said, his throat tightening with emotion. 'I really appreciate it.'

'I know you do, honey. I just wish she were a little more present.'

Morton fished in his pocket for one of his business cards. 'I know you can't say too much, but perhaps you could drop me an email every once in a while, to tell me how things are.'

'No problem—poor Velda don't get no visitors—so I'm glad *someone's* taking an interest in her.'

'What, no visitors at all?' Morton asked, slightly appalled.

Diane shook her head. 'None.'

'Fits with the way your aunt is,' Juliette mumbled.

'Right…' Morton's sentence tapered off and he offered Diane his hand to shake.

'Pleasure to meet you. Follow me,' she said, leading them back over to the reception desk to sign out.

Morton left the building, overwhelmed by a peculiar concoction of emotions that brought hot, bittersweet tears to his eyes. The great satisfaction at having finally met his grandmother was barbed with her debilitating illness, which had inevitably tarnished the occasion. Any hopes that he had held of her being able to help him find his father were wholly obliterated. Could he even take anything from what she had said about her being sorry for what she'd done?

Then there was the revelation that nobody visited her, which wrenched at his core.

Juliette instinctively pulled him into an embrace, as the tears broke free and coursed down his cheeks.

Chapter Ten

21ˢᵗ November 1950, Cow Hollow, San Francisco, California, USA

Velda woke slowly. For the past two weeks, the transition from sleep to waking had been difficult. Sometimes the unspeakable terrors playing out in her nightmares were eased by the opening of her eyes; other times the agonising process of surfacing from sleep and facing reality was excruciating, as she desperately tried to hold onto the thin, wispy hopes that had been contained in her dreams, as though she were wafting a net around, trying to catch something translucent and ultimately intangible.

Today, the simple natural act of waking up had been like the collision of two great planets. She had dreamed of the bridge again. Her mother was there, standing in the centre on the outer edge, beckoning her over. There was a wind—terribly loud—that snatched her mother's final words as she spoke them. Velda had moved closer and closer, desperate to hear what she had to say to explain herself. The closer she got to her mother, the noisier the wind became. Her mother's auburn hair was billowing furiously, as she tried to mouth the words more clearly. The dream ended as it always did: with her mother tumbling backwards, followed by darkness. Just total darkness.

Velda began to sob before she had even opened her eyes. She knew where she was—she was no longer on the bridge; she was in her bed. Alone. She had lost Joseph again, only this time he was irretrievably gone. Two weeks ago, Joseph's brother David had knocked on her door. She had known from the acute sadness that had contorted his face and his inability to speak that something had happened to Joseph. Something terrible.

'David? What is it?' Velda had pleaded.

He had handed over a telegram, still unable to speak. *It is with deep regret that I officially inform you that your son Sergeant First Class Joseph Jacklin has been missing since November 1ˢᵗ, 1950 as the result of participating in Korean operations. A letter containing further details will be forwarded to you at the earliest possible date. Please accept my sincere sympathy during this time of anxiety. Major General Charles H McCormack.*

Whilst those around her had sagged down in sobbing, boneless heaps, Velda had been consumed with an ugly rage that had first reared its head following her mother's death. Crushed by the vision of a future now lost, she had vented her anger on the house. In the handful of seconds before she had been restrained, anything within Velda's reach had been obliterated. Tables had been turned over. Chairs had cracked the sitting room windows. The lower panels of internal doors had been kicked in. Ornaments and vases had lain in hundreds of pieces on the wooden floor.

'Velda, stop crying and sit up. You need to take your pills,' her sister, Beatrice said, handing her a handkerchief.

Velda wiped her eyes and opened them fully for the first time this morning. The wilting dread of another day hit her. Take her barbiturates. Take a bath. Take a walk. Back to bed. Doctor's orders.

Beatrice was standing beside her, that same caring but supercilious smile looking down on her, as it had done ever since their mother had died in 1945. She was barely a year older than Velda, and yet had slipped somehow effortlessly into their late mother's vacant role.

'Here you go,' Beatrice said, her uncurled fingers revealing the plump pink pill that Velda had to take twice a day. In her other hand was a glass of water.

Velda swallowed down the pill and watched expressionlessly as Beatrice pulled open the curtains. She needn't have bothered—outside was a solid mass of drizzly grey.

'We'll need an umbrella for our walk today,' Beatrice said brightly.

'You can go by yourself,' Velda uttered.

Beatrice emitted a short laugh. 'Oh, come on; the fresh air will do you the world of good.'

'You don't actually want to go out in that, Beatrice,' Velda replied. She had heard the doctor's orders—that she shouldn't be left alone—spoken over her in bed, as though she were some kind of uncomprehending infant.

'Of course I do,' she retorted, trotting over to Velda's wardrobe and pulling open one of the doors. 'How about this today?' Beatrice held out a blue and white gingham dress. 'I've always loved this one.'

'Sure,' Velda said dismissively. She had learned that it was easier to just accept Beatrice's suggestions rather than to question them.

'Excellent—do you want me to help you get dressed?'

'I can manage,' Velda answered.

'See you downstairs, then,' Beatrice said. With a twirl of her skirt, she left the room.

She took her time getting ready. What was the hurry? She dressed, brushed her teeth and styled her hair—but for what, or whom? It did her good, Beatrice always insisted, to make herself presentable and take care of her appearance. Downstairs, she found a cup of coffee waiting for her and Beatrice sitting upright with her chest pushed outwards, her face beaming. How she maintained this constant sunny disposition was beyond Velda's understanding.

Velda went towards her usual armchair but Beatrice raised a hand. 'Don't sit down—you've got a guest.'

'Where? Who?'

'In the dining room. It's David Jacklin.'

'Oh my God,' Velda muttered, the blood draining from her face. She suddenly felt weak and fragile, as if she were made of thin glass that might shatter at any moment.

'Stay calm—I think it's good news.'

'What?'

'Go see him.'

Velda's legs were feathery and light, yet they managed to carry her across the hallway to the dining room. David stood from a chair with a wide grin on his face.

'Velda! He's alive! Joseph's alive!'

'Are you kidding?' Velda yelled.

David held up a thick envelope. 'We had this from him today—he's coming home!'

Velda burst into tears and threw her arms around him. Joseph was alive and well. A thick dark shroud, that she hadn't been aware had been encasing her body, suddenly fell away from her.

Her heart breathed again.

David broke their embrace and opened the envelope. 'Here—there's a letter for you.'

'For me?' Velda snatched the letter. She studied her name, scribed in his beautiful handwriting.

'Well, aren't you going to open it?' David laughed.

Velda took her time slicing into the envelope. Inside was a single sheet, short. *My Dear Velda, Contrary to popular belief I'm actually alive. I've got a few holes where I shouldn't have, but I'm still here. Listen, Velda, I know I should have listened to you. My time out here and all that's gone on has taught me a few things. When I get home I'm going to divorce Audrey. I'm not expecting you to come running back, but it's just something I need to do. I hope you're taking good care of yourself. Yours, Joseph.*

'What's he saying?' David asked, craning his neck to get a glimpse of the letter.

Velda folded it over and smiled. 'Nothing that concerns you, David Jacklin.'

'Okay. Well, I'll leave you to it—I'm Joseph's postman today—I've got a few more deliveries to make. Next stop Audrey's house.' David grimaced. 'I'm not sure how the news is going to go down over there.'

'Audrey?' Velda enquired, finally looking up from the envelope. 'I can take hers for you—I'm going out that way.'

'You sure? It's the other side of town.'

Velda smiled. 'Absolutely—Beatrice and I were just about to leave.' Velda extended her hand for the letter.

David opened the packet, then stopped. 'You *despise* Audrey. Are you really going to pass it on to her?'

'Sure I will.'

David raised his eyebrows.

'I'll go there right away—once I've made a fresh coffee—my last one will be ice by now.'

'If you're sure and you promise to give it to her.'

'Yes, I promise.'

David reluctantly handed over the letter. 'See you later, then.'

'Goodbye, David.'

'Bye, Velda. Take care now.'

Velda clutched both letters in her hand, waiting for the gentle *click* that indicated the closing of the front door and David's departure. When it arrived, she hurried back into the kitchen and filled the aluminium kettle with water.

'Well?' Beatrice asked, appearing at the doorway, eying the letters in her hand. 'I take it, it was good news about Joseph?'

Velda nodded. 'The best—he's coming home.'

'That's wonderful news—is he okay?'

'I think he got hurt, but he's okay.' She rushed over to Beatrice and hugged her tightly, continuing to cry. 'He's alive, Bea!'

Beatrice held her sister then said, 'He is still married, though, Velda.'

'I know.' Velda carefully set the letters down, hers covering Audrey's. 'Why don't you go and run yourself a nice bath before we go for that walk? I need a coffee and time to digest the news.'

Beatrice looked at the clock. 'At this time of the morning? What an indulgence.'

'Exactly,' Velda replied. She took her sister's hands in hers and met her gaze. 'Listen, Beatrice,' she began earnestly. 'The last couple of weeks have been—without the obvious exception—the worst in my life; I hit the bottom and you helped me through it and I can't thank you enough. Right now, I would just like a few minutes to myself to take it all in. Then, we can go for that walk. Hell, we can run, sing and dance, Beatrice!'

'Well…okay, then,' she agreed. 'If you're sure.'

'Positive,' Velda said, reaching up and pecking her sister on the cheek.

Beatrice fluttered from the room.

Velda wiped her face on her handkerchief and waited until she heard the tell-tale sounds of movement upstairs before she returned to the kettle. Switching it on to boil, she slid Audrey's letter out from beneath hers and held it in her hands, wondering as to the contents.

The thin pirouettes of steam that rose from the kettle spout began to grow more agitated and intense. Velda carefully held the envelope over the frantic surge of hot haze, watching as the gum became tacky. Small hillocks rose as the envelope flap began to separate.

Switching off the kettle, Velda took a butter knife from the drawer and carefully slid it along the V-shaped seam. The knife slid through the gum line effortlessly.

With vengeful satisfaction etched on her face, she took the letter out. Like hers, it was short. She read it quickly, but digested every word, then placed it back inside the envelope and pressed down on the top flap.

The letter was resealed, giving no indication that it had ever been opened.

With the envelope in her hand, Velda quietly slipped from the house.

It sure was some place for their first home after marrying. Typical Audrey. She had chosen an expensive place on 25th Avenue with exceptional views over the bay.

Velda stood at the porch and rang the doorbell, trying to suppress the feelings of disgust and loathing. Trying to suppress her anger.

The solid oak door opened and there, with her arms folded and lips pouting, stood Audrey. She was wearing a cream satin nightdress and movie-perfect make-up. 'Oh.'

'Audrey,' Velda smirked. 'How are you?'

Audrey rolled her eyes. 'Managing.'

'Yes, I saw you back in the summer. You were managing quite well with Dwight Kalinski.'

Audrey threw her head back in mock laughter. 'Oh, you really are a funny girl, you know. I can see why Joseph found you an amusing little thing. Such a shame he dumped you.'

Velda ignored the tingling onset of fury that pricked at her heart and handed over the letter.

Audrey stared at it like she was being handed a plate of excrement. *She didn't even recognise her own husband's handwriting.* 'It's for you.'

'What is it?' she sneered.

'A letter.'

'How witty of you. Is it from you? Some charming little outpouring of your ill feeling towards me?' Audrey laughed and pushed the door shut.

'It's from Joseph,' Velda stated, her voice raised. 'He's alive.'

The door reopened. Audrey drew in a long breath, staring at Velda.

'He wants a divorce,' Velda said with glee, flicking the letter out of Audrey's reach.

Audrey stretched across to grab the letter and, as she did so, her nightdress came open and Velda gasped.

Audrey pulled the nightdress closed, snatched the letter and slammed the door.

Velda had a wide grin on her face as she sauntered off the property, certain that she was being watched leave. Audrey was pregnant. Two or three months—four at the most. Joseph had been on the other side of the world for five months.

As she reached the sidewalk, Velda did a dramatic twirl and laughed back at the house.

Chapter Eleven

20th June 1976, Lothrop Hill Cemetery, Barnstable, Massachusetts, USA

The sky was a bright monotone blue. Cloudless. Hot. Jack's bare torso glistened with perspiration, as he toiled under the late afternoon sun. The thick black rubber gloves which he was forced to wear only added to his discomfort.

He dipped his sponge back into the murky bucket, then began to rub small circles to the rear of the headstone upon which he worked. The liquid—a pungent concoction of ammonium hydroxide and water—trickled down the dry grey headstone. Jack took a light brush and gently began to scrub away the effects of decades of grime and neglect. Inch by inch, the life and original colour returned to the stone.

Jack stood up and looked at the grave. It was for the son of the Reverend John Lothrop, the founder of the town of Barnstable. The words carved into the stone were once again legible. *Here lyes buried ye body of Mr John Lothrop who dec'd Sept ye 18th 1727 in the 85th year of his age.*

Slowly scanning around the cemetery, Jack took in the scale of his work. The place looked as if it were newly consecrated. The weeds had been all but completely eradicated and he had now cleaned up around a quarter of the headstones. Just another month or so and he could move onto phase three: the research.

A low rumble of a slowing car drew Jack's attention to the road. It was Mr Chipman's green Chrysler. Jack looked at his watch: just after five. Time to collect his wages, pack up and go to his American History evening class in West Barnstable. Jack waved as Mr Chipman entered the cemetery.

'Hey—wow—good work, Jack,' Mr Chipman said, glancing around the place. 'Looks amazing.'

'Thanks,' Jack replied, running the back of his hand over his sweaty forehead.

As Mr Chipman approached, he pulled out a roll of cash from his pocket. 'Here you go. I've taken out the box money already.'

'Thank you,' Jack said, taking the proffered roll of cash.

Mr Chipman then held aloft a piece of folded paper and grimaced. 'I've got some information.'

'What about?' Jack asked.

'Your dad—his past.'

Jack frowned. 'But I told you that you could stop all that back in March—my mom explained everything to me.'

'I know, I know—I'll take it away and destroy it if you want,' Mr Chipman said. 'I did stop digging—but I neglected to inform an old colleague of mine back in California that the search was off. He found something that I thought you might want to see.'

Jack shook his head. He didn't want to reignite the embers of his mistrust. Since his mom had caught him leaving his dad's study, things had returned to normal at home. She had confronted him that day with a surprising calmness.

'What are you doing, Jack?' she had asked.

Momentarily caught in a frozen terror, Jack had said nothing. He had considered lying—perhaps making something up about needing money—but then he had stopped that line of thinking dead; it was a whole patchwork quilt of lies from his mom and dad that he was now trying to unstitch. Truth was the only option. 'I phoned the bank pretending to be dad,' he had begun. 'He gets a bunch of money in every month from San Francisco, which I believe comes from some inheritance or other. I think Dad was born there, not in Boston.'

His mom's face had turned a deeper shade of pink, but other than that, she had kept her reaction guarded, reserved. 'Okay, I think it's time to explain, Jack,' she had said quietly. 'Come and sit down with me.'

His mom had sat opposite him at the kitchen table, her hands clasped piously together. 'The truth is, your dad doesn't know *where* he's from. His mother—and I am sorry for speaking ill of the dead—was something of a loose woman and gave your dad up as a young baby. Can you imagine your dad—Vice President of the Cape Cod Chamber of Commerce—admitting to people, his own family, that he knows nothing of his past? He lied—yes—and that was wrong—but it was just easier to say that he was from Boston and that his parents were killed in an automobile accident. Do you see that, Jack?'

Jack had trusted his mother's mournful eyes. He nodded. 'Yeah, I guess so. But where does the money come from, then?'

His mom had laughed. 'Investments—your dad isn't as dumb as he makes out, you know.'

Jack had smiled and his mom had reached across the table and touched his hand. 'Listen, Jack, I won't tell him that you were in there, or about our little discussion, okay?'

'Thank you,' he had said. The past life, that he had imagined for his dad, suddenly seemed as foolish and absurd as the idiotic ones that he and Alice had dreamed up a couple of years ago.

'Jack?' Mr Chipman repeated. 'What do you want me to do with this?' He waved the sheet of paper in front of Jack's eyes.

The words were dry in his mouth: destroy it. They were right there, sitting obstinately on his tongue. *Destroy it*. But he couldn't vocalise them; they clashed with an imprecise but forceful intensity within him that kept his mouth clamped shut. *Destroy it*. It was his mom's voice, he realised, encouraging him to say it. 'Does it contradict what my mom told me?' Jack breathed.

Mr Chipman nodded. It was a slow, apologetic nod of his head. His eyes fell to the floor. 'Quite a dilemma for you.'

'What would you do?' Jack asked.

'I'll answer that after you do,' he said.

'Show me.'

'You're sure?'

'No, but show me anyway. I'd spend my whole life wondering; I need to know.'

Mr Chipman silently unfolded the sheet of paper and held it out in Jack's direction. It was a Xerox copy, covered in an old style of handwriting. Jack pushed his face closer to the paper. On the left-hand side was a long list of names. All men. He scanned down until he found a familiar surname. Jas. Jacklin. The next column listed ages. Nineteen. Next, judging by the content, were the men's occupations. Jas.—James Jacklin—was, like many on the list, a miner. Lastly, was a place name: Pennsylvania.

'James Jacklin?' Jack queried. 'Who's he?'

'Your great-great-great-grandfather.'

'Okay,' Jack said. So far, nothing that refuted his mom's version of events.

'This is the 1850 census. He was your first ancestor to live in California. Notice where he's living?'

'In a hotel with a bunch of other men from all over the world.'

'Look at the place, at the top.'

'Coloma?'

Mr Chipman opened his hands out and pulled a face that suggested the place should be familiar to Jack. 'Come on, Jack! 1850. California.'

'Gold Rush?' Jack said tentatively.

'Exactly.'

Jack was perplexed. 'So my great-great-great-grandfather, James Jacklin was born in Pennsylvania but travelled to California for the Gold Rush?'

'That's right.'

'So…'

Mr Chipman flipped the page over to reveal a hand-drawn family tree. 'There's you at the bottom here.' His finger traced from Jack up to his dad. 'And here's your dad. He was born in San Francisco. Just like his father, George and George's father and his father and his father.'

Jack's mom and dad's version of events was a lie. His mom's cover of his dad's version of events was a lie. The unpalatable truth was documented here. Unassailable history.

'There's something else, too,' Mr Chipman added. 'Take a look at your grandfather on the tree.'

Jack scrutinised the family tree. 'George Jacklin. Born 1900. Married Lucy Bradford.' He looked at Mr Chipman for further direction.

'When did he die?' Mr Chipman asked.

'It doesn't say.'

'That's because he's still alive, Jack.'

'What?'

'He and your grandmother, Lucy and your uncle David—they're all alive and living in San Francisco.' He took something—a scrap of paper—from his pocket and handed it to Jack. 'Here's their address—quite a wealthy part of town, so I'm told.'

'But I just can't believe this…' Jack's sentence was jerked into the collision of thoughts ricocheting around his mind. His grandparents were still alive. He heard Mr Chipman talking—saying something about the need to discuss things with his parents.

'Oh, and one other thing,' Mr Chipman said. 'What you were told about your mom's parents—that was true. Her father died in 1932 and her mother in 1945.'

The way that Mr Chipman relayed the news of his maternal grandparents was as though it might have been of some consolation that at least some part of their past had been true. It wasn't; it just made everything more complex, somehow.

'Thank you,' Jack heard himself saying. 'I'd better get packed up and off to school.'

'Ask them to teach you about the Gold Rush,' Mr Chipman joked.

Jack smiled absentmindedly and watched as Mr Chipman strolled through the cemetery towards the gates, his mind in freefall.

'I would have looked at the papers, too, by the way!' Mr Chipman called back down.

Jack pulled up on the drive and killed the engine. He stared at his parents' house in a detached way, as if seeing it for the first time. Through the thin bands of the horizontal blinds, he saw his dad reading, silhouetted against the vanilla dining-room lights. The astute businessman from humble Bostonian beginnings, now living in one of the nicest neighbourhoods on Cape Cod. The epitome of the American Dream.

Jack's gaze dropped to the passenger seat beside him to the evidence that annihilated everything he knew. A mild rage rose inside him.

Stuffing the sheet into his class folder, Jack climbed from the car and entered the house. He closed the door, hung up his coat and wandered casually into the dining room. He tried to behave normally, but it didn't come easily. 'Hi,' he said.

His dad looked up from the newspaper. 'Hi. How did school go tonight?'

'Good thanks. I learned quite a lot today about the California Gold Rush.'

'Interesting period,' his dad mumbled, turning back to his newspaper.

'Ever go?' Jack asked.

'To California? No, too hot.'

Jack placed his folder on the table and turned to get something to drink.

'What's this?' his dad asked. His face was ashen, drained. His jaw was clenched and the hand that was holding the paper on which was drawn the Jacklin family tree trembled.

His dad had taken the bait.

'What have you done, Jack?' The tremor that Jack had glimpsed in his dad's hand was progressively engulfing him. It squeezed his voice box, pinched his eyes and crushed his breath.

In that instance, Jack knew that he had gone too far. He had opened a hidden window onto the past, a window that offered a view of the ugly chasm between his dad's two lives. A window that could never again be closed.

His dad pushed back his chair, rushed over to Jack and, with an animalistic roar, shoved Jack backwards, pinning him against the wall by his throat.

'Please!' Jack begged.

'Who do you think you are?' his dad seethed.

'That's just what I want to know,' Jack tried to argue, but the pressure on his throat was increasing and he was struggling to breathe. He had no choice and drove his right knee up into his dad's stomach.

It worked. His dad let him go but, giving him no chance to blink, he heaved his fist into Jack's face. There was the sound akin to a stick being snapped, as his knuckles met with Jack's nose.

Jack fell to the floor in agony and curled himself up in the foetal position. 'Please! I just want to understand…' he began to say, but the sharp jolt of his dad's foot into his stomach thrust the breath from his lungs and tore the words apart.

Chapter Twelve

20th August 2016, Wellfleet, Massachusetts, USA

'It's kind of how I imagined it,' Morton said. He was standing beside Juliette in the car park adjacent to the First Congregational Church in Wellfleet: the place of his grandparents' 1953 marriage. It was a large colonial-style building cladded in the typical New England white boarding. He slowly walked around to the front of the church, up the three red-brick steps to the double doors and tried the handle. Locked. With his back to the doors and his hands slung in his pockets, he pictured his grandfather standing on this very spot, looking down a street that had changed little in the intervening sixty years. Old, white homes interspersed with thick trees; just as it had always been.

The raft of unanswered questions began to resurface in his thoughts. Questions that he might just get some answers to today. They were on their way back up the Cape towards Provincetown, to go to his Aunt Alice's house. Yesterday, whilst he and Juliette were enjoying a very pleasant bicycle ride along the Cape Cod Rail Trail—a twenty-two-mile former railroad track—his mobile had rung with an American number. 'Hi there, is that Morton?' a female voice had asked.

'Speaking.'

'Oh, hi. This is Jan—I saw you briefly yesterday at *Alice's Art*.'

'Okay,' he had said, not having the first clue with whom he was speaking.

'Alice—she's my wife. I'm really sorry for her bluntness. She's very mistrusting,' Jan had said with a laugh. 'Listen, do you guys want to come over to our house tomorrow night?'

'Yes, we'd love to,' Morton had answered. 'Is Alice okay with that?'

The line had gone silent for several seconds. 'Let's just say I'm working on it, but I'm getting there. We live at sixty-two Commercial Street. Come by around eight o'clock and we'll have a wine or beer together.'

'Ready?' Juliette asked. 'If we don't get a move on, we won't have time to eat before going to see your aunt.'

'Yeah, let's go,' he replied, leading away from the church and back to the hire car. 'But what if Jan hasn't managed to convince Alice that seeing us is a good idea?' He faced Juliette as he started the car.

'I'm guessing Jan would have called you back and cancelled.'

'Call me sceptical, but I just can't see her welcoming me with open arms.'

'Well, we'll find out in a couple of hours.'

'Great.'

They had eaten out in the front of Bubala's by the Bay—a sprawling restaurant that, just like Commercial Street that ran beside it, was bustling with young revellers enjoying the last of the warm Provincetown evening sunshine. Their table had been cleared and the bill had been paid.

Morton looked at his watch. 'Quarter to eight—I guess we'd better be leaving.' He sank the final swig of his red wine, the effects of which had temporarily doused the sparks of niggling worries and the questioning of the wisdom of their decision. But really, what choice did he have? Other than to pursue online the higher echelons of his family tree in San Francisco, he had no further leads to track down his father.

His mood was cautiously light as they left the restaurant and made their way further along Commercial Street.

As the shops, galleries and restaurants grew fewer, so the crowds also diminished.

'There it is,' Juliette announced after some time, a note of finality to her voice.

Morton stopped outside the gate of number sixty-two Commercial Street. Cladded in orange cedar wood tiles, the house stood ostentatiously against its white weather-boarded neighbours. A short brick path led to the front door, which was set in the centre of the house, dividing two identical gabled fronts.

Juliette pushed open the gate and led the way. She pressed the bell, then took a step back.

It was Jan who answered, and Morton then remembered her from the hut on MacMillan Pier. She smiled warmly. 'Hi, guys, come on in.'

Morton stepped into the house and offered his hand. 'We weren't properly introduced—I'm Morton; this is my wife, Juliette.'

'Welcome,' Jan said, shaking their hands vigorously. 'Come on through.'

Morton glanced around the hallway—obviously the home of an artist—the white walls were filled with an abundance of nautical-themed art work and sculptures. They walked under a giant tin and copper seahorse to enter the sitting room at the rear of the house.

'Wow,' Juliette gasped.

'Impressive,' Morton concurred. The bi-folding doors were open to a large deck. A glass balcony provided a seamless join between house and ocean.

'Come on out,' Jan said. 'Alice will be down in a moment.'

They followed her out to the edge of the deck and looked out over at the sandy beach below them. Small waves hesitantly licked the braid of black seaweed that meandered its way along the shoreline.

Morton stared at what he considered to be one of the most fantastic sunsets that he had ever seen. A pudgy tangerine sun, with its lower edge dipped in the ocean, gave off an inert medley of every shade of red and yellow imaginable. For the briefest of moments, he forgot all about their reason for being here. Then he remembered. 'Is Alice okay with all this?' he whispered to Jan.

'Yeah. She's a typical artist—likes to be a bit reclusive and mysterious—you know the sort,' Jan said with a laugh.

'I can see why—I don't think I'd ever want to leave this house with that view,' Juliette commented.

'That's why the place is a haven for artists—it has the most perfect light here all year round. Even in winter, when all the tourists have returned home and most of the shops and restaurants have closed, it's an amazing place.'

'It seems pretty special,' Morton agreed, suddenly feeling his heart lurch and a nervous tingle rising inside him, as he sensed someone approaching from behind. He turned around to see her—his bohemian Aunt Alice. She was wearing a lavender-coloured kaftan and her wild hair was swept back behind a headband.

'Hello again,' Alice greeted.

'Hello,' Morton said, still unsure of exactly what to say. Jan being the one who had invited them meant that it clearly wasn't Alice's idea. Had she been browbeaten into accepting them into her home? What did that mean for their topics of conversation? Could he ask about his father, given how she had treated him?

Alice seemed to study him for an age. 'You look a lot like him,' she said finally. 'I'm sorry for how I was the other day—you caught me off-guard. I'm Alice.' She extended her hand, which Morton accepted with a smile.

'Morton—and this is my wife, Juliette.'

'Nice to meet you,' Alice greeted, shaking Juliette's hand.

'Thank you for seeing us,' Juliette said.

'Well, you're family,' Jan responded. 'And what do you folks like to drink? Wine? Beer? English tea?'

'Wine would be great for both of us—thank you,' Morton answered.

'Come and sit down,' Alice said, directing them to a table and chairs on the deck. 'I guess we've got a lot of catching up to do…'

The three of them sat at the table while Jan disappeared inside the house.

A silence peculiar to their situation settled uncomfortably between them. There was so much to say, yet Morton couldn't find a way to begin.

'How long have you lived here?' Juliette asked, breaking the stalemate.

Alice tipped her head back, as if it were a difficult question. 'We settled here twenty-something years ago, now.'

'We live in Rye in East Sussex—I don't know if you've ever heard of it?' Juliette asked, taking a sideways glance at Morton.

Alice thought for a moment then shook her head. 'No, can't say I have. I've never been to England. The one time my parents went, they left me behind.'

Morton had found his way in. 'But they took your brother,' he said. His words came out slightly stilted, sounding neither like a question, nor a statement.

'Yes, that's right,' Alice answered. 'Which I guess is when he met your mother?'

'Yes, my biological mother was living next door to the guesthouse in Folkestone where your parents and brother came to stay for the week in January 1974.'

'Here we go,' Jan chimed, walking over and carefully placing a tray on the table. She poured four glasses of red wine, then distributed them out. 'Cheers,' she toasted. 'To long-lost family.'

'To long-lost family,' they all echoed.

Jan took a seat and addressed Morton. 'I'm real curious about your story—I've got so many questions! So, you found out later in life that you were adopted and then set about finding your real parents, is that right?'

'Yes, that's right. It turns out that my adoptive father's sister was actually my biological mother.'

Jan's eyes rolled heavenwards as she repeated him. 'Your adoptive father's sister was your biological mother. Right, okay—I think I'm with you. Golly—tell us everything!'

And so he did. His Aunt Alice sat impassively, whilst Jan made all the appropriate noises and responses expected from his story. He told them how he had tracked down a visitors' book that had once belonged to the owners of the guesthouse that his father had visited, which in turn had led to a raft of online documents, including the birth record of both his father and his Aunt Alice. He also told them of some of his discoveries since being in America. He omitted to mention anything of Alice's father's first marriage, or the connection to California. How much—if anything—did she know? He ended his long account by handing them copies of the letters his father had written to his mother in 1976.

'I deliberated for so long about what to do with them...' Morton said, feeling as though he needed to explain himself, as he handed them to Alice.

Nobody spoke while she read the first letter.

Morton tried to read her face, but she gave nothing away. She passed the letter over to Jan and opened the second.

Alice swallowed hard and Morton noticed that her eyes were slightly wet. Saying nothing, she put the letter back in the envelope and handed it to Jan. She read the third letter in the same way—revealing nothing.

'Awful,' Jan commented, once she had finished the letters. 'Just awful.'

Morton looked at Alice and decided that he needed to tackle the problem head-on. 'Do you know where my father went after the fire?'

'He stayed for a while with friends then left town. He never came back.'

'He stayed with the Chipman family, didn't he?' Morton probed.

'Yes, that's right,' Alice confirmed.

'I believe that Michael Chipman died in 2007—do you know what happened to Laura, his twin sister?' Morton asked.

Alice took a long inhalation before speaking. 'She moved to Canada.'

'Do you know when, or to which part she went?' Morton asked.

Alice thought for a moment. 'Alberta, I believe. It must have been around 1982.'

'And do you know if she married—so I can try and trace her?'

'She did, but she kept her own name,' Alice answered.

'That makes things a little easier,' Morton said, scribbling notes onto his pad. He wrote the word *fire* then underlined it. How was he going to ask what had actually happened on that Christmas Eve in 1976? Directly, he decided. 'Do you mind talking about the fire?'

He heard her quickly draw breath. 'No, I guess not. I'm not sure how it will help find my brother... What is it you want to know, exactly?'

'Just what happened. Where was Jack when the fire started?'

She seemed to take an age to organise her thoughts and answer his question. 'Jack and I were up in my room—chatting as we did most evenings after dinner. As you know, it was Christmas Eve, so we were expecting to be called downstairs to play board games. We left my dad to go and get them in the basement, while my mom was moving presents from her bedroom to the sitting room. We heard her passing my door several times then she just screamed. We ran out into the hall to see smoke billowing up the stairs and fire shooting out of the sitting room. We used Jack's bedroom window to escape. Us three made it out, but my dad didn't.'

'And you were injured?' Morton asked.

'Yeah,' Alice answered, glancing down at her left arm. 'I tried to find Dad...but he was in the basement and I just couldn't reach him.'

'So what caused the fire?'

'Some electrical fault with the Christmas tree lights.'

'But why, then, in the final letter from your brother, did he say your mum blamed him for it?' Morton asked, taking a sip of wine.

'I don't know—things had been really tense between Jack and Mom and Dad for a few months. I think things came to a head that night and they got into a bit of a fight—just before the fire.'

It still didn't make sense to Morton. He was certain that Alice was withholding information. 'Do you know what they were fighting about?'

Alice shook her head. 'No—probably normal teenager stuff. After that, he just took off.'

'Did you never wonder what happened to him?' Juliette quizzed, the policewoman in her making an appearance.

'Sure I did, but it was his choice. After what happened I understand that he wants to be left alone.'

The cutting nuance of her voice was palpable. Morton shot a look at Juliette, then caught Jan's uncomfortable shifting in her chair.

'Why don't you show Morton the bits that survived the fire?' Jan suggested to Alice, then turned to face him. 'There were a few pieces that survived—God only knows how.'

'Come to the front room,' Alice said.

'You two go,' Jan said to Morton with a sweeping swoosh of her hand. 'Juliette and I are going to stay here and enjoy the last of the sunset for a bit longer.'

Juliette smiled, sat back in her chair and drank more of her wine.

Morton heard Jan beginning to ask her questions about what she did for a living, as he trailed Alice back inside the house to a room at the front. Two of the walls had custom-made, floor-to-ceiling bookshelves crafted around the door and the front-facing window. The other two walls were covered in various works of art. Alice headed to one of the shelves, withdrew a book of some kind and handed it to Morton. 'One of my most treasured possessions,' she said almost inaudibly.

It was a photo album, light in his hands. That it had suffered in a fire was indisputable. The original tan leather was only visible in one small circular patch; the rest was tarnished with a charcoal residue that felt slightly greasy to the touch. Morton lifted it to his nose. He was able to detect the faintest whiff of acrid smoke. Having once lost a house in an explosion, it was a smell that he knew only too well. He placed the album down on an old-fashioned wooden school desk in front of the window and turned the first page.

'That's us,' Alice explained without emotion.

It was an informal photo that made Morton smile. He recognised the location—it was taken in the front garden of 2239 Iyanough Avenue. The house—pre-fire—was completely different to that which now stood in its place. Standing on the lawn was a man in a yellow shirt and brown trousers, whom he recognised as being his grandfather. In one arm, with her face towards the camera, was Alice. Morton estimated her to have been around the age of five. Beside them, looking at the two- or three-year-old Jack in her arms, was his grandmother, Velda.

'That was around 1959 or 1960,' Alice remarked. 'The earliest photo I have of anyone in the family. I guess that sounds crazy to a genealogist, right?'

'Frustrating more than crazy,' Morton responded. 'Do you mind if I take photos of the pictures?'

'Sure—go ahead.'

Having taken a photograph, he turned to the next double page. They contained an assortment of photos all taken at the beach. There was a close-up of his father, Jack, wearing swimming trunks and holding a beach ball. Another of Velda and the two kids paddling in the sea. Another—presumably taken by one of the children—of his grandparents with the tops of their heads missing.

'Hyannis, summer 1962,' Alice commented.

The next page contained more snapshots of visits to parks, zoos and beaches. As Morton took photos, Alice outlined the locations and dates.

'How are you folks getting on, then?' Jan asked, peering around the door.

'Lovely album,' Morton said. 'Thank goodness it survived.'

'Isn't it just,' Jan said, entering the room and looking over his shoulder. 'Oh, I just love that picture of my little Ali! How old were you, there?'

'About ten, I guess.'

Morton turned the page to see several photographs of his father posing outside the front of the house.

'His first day at Barnstable High School,' Alice said. 'He was so excited about it—he loved school—loved learning.'

'Really?' Morton said, getting his first snippet of his father's personality. 'What were his favourite subjects?'

'Art, history, math, literature—most things.' Alice smiled warmly—the first genuine smile of the evening, Morton believed.

'And what was he like at home? What were his hobbies, pastimes?'

'Like most boys, he liked his sports. Going out on his bike. Sailing. Sea fishing with our dad. Reading. As he got older, he was interested in archaeology, history—that kind of thing. He managed a couple of semesters at Boston, then dropped out.'

'To do what?' Morton asked.

'Shop work for a while—a grocery store on Main Street called Rory's. He quit that and then started working for Mr Chipman.'

'Really? Doing what?'

'Something up at Lothrop Hill Cemetery—maintaining the grounds—recording who was buried where—I don't know, exactly—it was all just before the fire.'

'Sounds like something I would do,' Morton remarked.

'Like father, like son,' Jan laughed.

'England,' Alice said when Morton turned the page. 'The last photos in the album are of their holiday to England in 1974.'

Morton scanned the images quickly, hoping to see one of his biological mother and father together, but there was none. The pictures were mainly of a day trip to London—Buckingham Palace, Big Ben, the River Thames and one of the royal parks. Others had been taken at landmarks that Morton recognised—Canterbury Cathedral, Dover Castle—there was even one taken on Mermaid Street in Rye—almost directly opposite Morton's house. It was a peculiar feeling to know that his father had once trodden the cobbles outside his home. 'I was hoping to see them together—my biological mother and father,' he said.

'Maybe one day you will,' Alice replied. 'You seem pretty tenacious in your investigations, I must say.'

'He's my father. I won't stop until I find him—dead or alive.' He faced Alice. 'Do you think you would have heard, if he had died?'

'I guess so...'

'I'm sure he's alive,' Jan added. 'Just keep looking. What else survived the fire, Ali?'

'Some ornaments, kitchen bits...' Alice listed. 'Nothing family-related.'

Morton turned back to the front of the album and studied the first image again. 'So, no photos of your parents before 1959?' he said, shoving a not-very-subtle crowbar into the conversation.

'Nope—not one,' Alice replied.

'What do you know about your mother and father before their marriage?' he questioned.

'Well, just before that he was fighting in Korea. He did some heroic thing or other and got sent home. He used to tell us that he was one of the first men to volunteer to fight.' Alice's face lightened at the memory. 'He used to place great emphasis on the *volunteered* part—and not being drafted. He and Mom married in 1953, then Jack and I came along.'

'What about *before* Korea?' Morton probed.

Alice folded her arms and met his gaze. 'You're asking about San Francisco, aren't you? And the first wife?'

Morton nodded. So she knew.

'It was Jack who found out—that's what he was talking about in the letters. Growing up, we had no idea. Mom and Dad had us believe they were from Boston. It drove Jack crazy and he needed to find the truth. And that's what he did—he found it. You're a lot like him.'

Morton smiled and she reached out and touched his arm.

'Come on, let's go back outside,' Jan said. 'Poor Juliette will think we've deserted her. She just told me you're on your honeymoon, Morton! Congratulations. Come and tell us all about how you two met.'

It was almost one o'clock in the morning when Morton and Juliette left. By the end of the evening, three pages of his notepad were filled with snapshots of his father's life: his favourite movie (*The Godfather*), favourite food (pizza), favourite colour (green), favourite music (The Beatles)—all of it frozen in time in 1976. But of his whereabouts, Morton had learned absolutely nothing more. He and Juliette hugged Alice and Jan and left the house with smiles and promises to keep in touch.

'Oh, I almost forgot—we've got you a gift to take back to England,' Jan called, as they began down the path. She scuttled inside and returned with the snow fence painting of a northern cardinal that Morton had picked up on MacMillan Pier.

'Thank you—I love it,' he said.

'It was your dad's favourite bird,' Alice revealed.

'Really?'

'Yeah, he used to feed them his lunch in the cemetery he worked in,' Alice remarked with a smile.

'Wow, thanks.'

The door closed behind them and Morton threaded his arm through Juliette's, as they made their way back down Commercial Street to their hire car. 'I'm sure she knows where he is,' Morton declared.

'Yes,' Juliette agreed.

'You think so, too?' He had expected her to challenge him on it—needing some kind of proof that he didn't have, it was just his gut instinct. 'Some of the things they said just didn't add up. And Alice slipped into the present tense a couple of times. *After what happened I understand that he wants to be left alone.*'

'Yeah, I noticed that.'

'Did you pick up on anything else? Or is it just your policewoman's hunch?'

'This,' Juliette said, holding her mobile phone in front of his face. It was a close-up picture of a man and a woman grinning at the camera.

The man was undoubtedly his father. It was a truly bizarre moment—seeing his biological father having aged in front of his eyes. His hair had flashes of grey and his nose was fractionally off-set.

'God…' Morton breathed.

'How old does he look there? Fifty? Sixty?'

'Which means it was taken sometime in the last ten years…' Morton said excitedly. 'That woman—is she famous…there's something familiar about her.'

'Not that I recognise, no.'

'Where did you find it?' Morton asked.

'When Jan went off to see what you and Alice were up to, I took a quick peek at their photos. It was on a bookshelf with some others but was the only one lying face down.'

'Really?'

'Yep—they clearly didn't want us to see it. He's alive, Morton.'

'Yes, but does he want to be found?'

Chapter Thirteen

4th December 1950, Cow Hollow, San Francisco, California, USA

Life couldn't get any more perfect. A winter sun shone through Velda's bedroom window, engulfing her in a halo of light. She was sitting at her table applying a light dusting of blue eyeshadow. She was no longer taking any medication and she felt amazing. Alive. She smiled at her reflection and headed for the door.

'*Another* new dress? Where are you going, all dolled up?' Beatrice asked when she arrived downstairs.

Velda did a twirl. 'This old thing?' she replied coyly. 'Do you like it?'

Beatrice raised an eyebrow. 'I'm guessing you're going to see *him*?'

Velda flounced. 'When are you going to start actually using his name?'

'Okay: I'm guessing you're going to see Mr Joseph Jacklin, Audrey's husband?' Beatrice corrected.

'Not for much longer—he's sorted out all the divorce paperwork. His attorney thinks it will all be done and dusted in the New Year. Then he'll be free to marry again.'

'I just hope you know what you're doing, Velda.'

'I do! I do!' Velda chimed as she waltzed out of the front door.

'Well, hi there, Velda,' Joseph's father greeted. 'Come on in. Joseph! You've got a visitor.'

'Thank you, George,' Velda said, entering the house.

Joseph, with a wide grin on his face, hobbled out from the dining room, which had been converted into his recovery room. He was walking unaided now, but still couldn't manage steps owing to the pieces of shrapnel lodged in his hip. 'My, don't you look swell.'

'You're looking better each day, too,' Velda commented.

Joseph leant in and kissed her on the cheek. 'Want to go for a walk?'

'Sure—if you're up to it?'

'It'll do me good,' Joseph said. He took his jacket from the coat-stand and opened the door for Velda. 'After you, ma'am.'

Velda curtseyed. 'Why thank you, kind sir.'

'Do you have anywhere you want to walk to?' he asked.

With Joseph at her side, she didn't care where she was in the world. 'I don't mind,' she replied, linking her arm through his.

They ambled slowly down the cold street. It was several seconds before either of them spoke.

'So, I should hear back from my attorney any day now. Audrey was given the divorce papers yesterday.'

Velda nodded but said nothing.

'Can you believe it—she's moved Dwight Kalinski into the house—*my* house—the house I'm paying for. I mean, of all the things. Can you believe it?'

Velda could believe it. It was Audrey Fuller they were talking about, after all. 'Expect the unexpected as far as *she's* concerned.'

'The woman just has no moral decency,' Joseph seethed.

'She'll get what's coming to her, one day,' Velda said.

'One thing's for certain—she hasn't got a legal leg to stand on—I've got a whole truck-load of witnesses who'll say she was carrying on with him behind my back, while I was out there fighting for my country—her country.'

'Almost dying for your country,' Velda corrected, gently stroking his arm. 'But I must say, you're recovering real well, Joseph. You'll be running around the block again in no time.'

'Just walking's good enough for me.'

'You're a tough one.'

'I think me being still alive is more to do with the accuracy of the gooks. Six bullets—all of them missing major organs and arteries—that's got to be some kind of record.' He took a long, appreciative breath and squeezed Velda's arm. 'Jeez, I'm glad to be back here. There are a whole bunch of guys out there who won't be so damn lucky.'

They walked without aim, ending up in a small café on Fillmore Street. Velda kept their conversation light, despite her yearning to discuss the future. People close to Joseph had implied that once divorced, he would likely waste no time in proposing to Velda. Her friends had begun to discuss the wedding. At first they had talked in loose, general terms, then specific dates, styles, floral arrangements and venues had been mooted. They had debated where the couple might live and how long they would wait before trying for their first child. Velda now found herself with a clear image of her wedding to Joseph in her head, despite his having never uttered a single word about it. Whenever they were alone together, a small part of her was anxiously anticipating his proposal.

'What do you say we go catch a movie?' Joseph suggested as they drank the last inches of their sodas.

'Sure—I'm in no hurry to get home.'

'Great—let's go.'

They left the Grand Theater on Mission Street just under two hours later, having watched *Destination Murder*.

'Well, I'm sure glad you didn't get any ideas from that movie,' Joseph chuckled.

Velda playfully slapped his arm. 'And what do you mean by that?'

Joseph shrugged and laughed. 'Woman ducks out from a movie theatre in the intermission, goes and murders someone then returns with her alibi intact.'

Velda's face scrunched into pretend thought. 'Hmm…could I get up to Twenty-Fifth Avenue and back in five minutes?'

They both laughed and began to stroll away from the theatre.

'Why did you do it, Joseph?' Velda asked, finally finding the courage to voice a question that had been bothering her since he had returned home. 'Why did you risk your life like that in Korea? You could so easily have been killed.'

Joseph took a moment to answer. 'You know what? The reason I joined up in the first place was to escape the mess at home—with Audrey, I mean. Out there I was free of it—didn't have to think. Do you know, Velda, she wrote me just once in the whole time I was out there? Once. So it was okay not to think about home—easy, even. Then the letters started coming—folk telling me what she was up to.'

'I'm sorry,' Velda said, a bubble of deep anger welling inside her. She had been one of those letter-writers.

'Anyway, things started playing on my mind all the time and there was nothing I could do about it, you know? That day…the day that it happened…I wasn't myself…I wasn't concentrating. Me and the other guys got ourselves pinned into a corner and I was shot in the arm,' he said, touching his right bicep. 'We were like sitting ducks—waiting to be killed. I knew the only thing that could save us was one of us making it to the machinegun emplacement and I just couldn't ask it of the other guys. At that moment I just saw clarity—complete clarity: if I made it to the gun me and the other guys would live; if I died then I got myself a way out of the mess at home.' He emitted an ironic kind of laugh. 'It's funny—I get a medal for bravery but actually it was driven by cowardice.'

Velda squeezed his arm. 'Of course it's not cowardice—you wanted to *save* the men around you and you did. You made it to the machinegun.'

'And received another five bullets in the process and had to kill three men.'

'That must have been hard…'

'It was like nothing else. It sure is a strange quirk of humanity—there's nothing—no amount of money—nothing—that could make me take someone's life.' He gestured to the people wandering the sidewalk in his view. 'I just couldn't do it. And yet out there, in a war when it's kill or be killed, I didn't have a problem. A bullet in each of their heads and bayonet through the chest of the third one. I saw the life leave their eyes and felt nothing but relief…I don't know what kind of a man that makes me, Velda, I really don't.'

'It makes you just a man, Joseph. Normal in many ways, exceptional in others. *My* Joseph Jacklin.'

Joseph smiled. 'And that was it. The guys survived and I blacked out. Next thing I know, I'm in an army hospital being prepared to return home.'

'My hero,' Velda said.

They had reached his house. 'Well, do you want to come in for some dinner?'

Velda nodded. 'I'd love that.' She followed Joseph inside his house.

'What say we put some records on and I try some dancing?' he suggested, moving his arms and legs in a stiff, robotic way.

Velda laughed.

'Joseph.' It was his father, appearing from the sitting room door, his face grave. 'Mr Segghetti's here,' he whispered.

'Okay.'

Velda could see that it wasn't the good news they had been expecting. Joseph faced Velda. 'We'll take a rain check on dinner and dancing. I'll see you later.' He walked alongside his father towards the sitting room.

'Let me come in, too,' Velda pleaded.

Joseph shot a look to his father and thought for a second. 'Okay.'

Mr Segghetti, a rotund man with an ill-fitting black suit, stood to shake Joseph's hand as they entered the sitting room. Despite his dubious appearance, he was apparently one of the best divorce attorneys in the city.

'Mr Segghetti—this is my good friend, Velda,' Joseph introduced.

'Ah,' Mr Segghetti said, taking Velda's hand in his. 'It's a pleasure.'

Velda smiled and retracted her hand from his sweaty grip. Was she reading into it, or had there been some trace of recognition in his voice? Had Joseph told him of his intention to marry again? Or had her name cropped up somehow in the divorce paperwork? She kept her composure and stood primly on the outskirts of the conversation.

'She won't accept the terms,' Mr Segghetti said.

Joseph nodded. It was what he had anticipated. It was what they had all anticipated. 'Okay, up the offer.'

'I did—several times.'

'Up it some more, then,' Joseph yelled.

'Mr Jacklin—I've presented terms to her attorney that I have *never* offered before in my career—she won't take it.'

Joseph blew out a puff of air. 'Then ask what *her* terms are.'

'Mr Jacklin—you're not understanding me—she has no terms; she won't divorce you. If you have plans for the future—' he glanced quickly at Velda '—then you're going to have to rethink them.'

The bubble of anger inside Velda erupted uncontrollably. 'Damn Audrey!' she ranted, picking up a cup from the table and launching it at the wall. Dark coffee tears streamed down the flowery silk wallpaper, meeting the shards of bone china on the carpet below.

'Velda!' Joseph stammered, stretching out to grab her hand, as she reached for another cup to launch. 'Stop! Can't you see, this is what she wants?'

But Velda couldn't see anything but that evil bitch's face smirking; that she once again held the upper hand. The rage ravaged her body like a fever. She felt a tight grip on her wrists. She was being pushed down into a chair. Held there while a tirade of curses and invectives spewed from her mouth.

Her eyes were playing tricks on her. The room was dark but a slice of light cut through—found its way through what? A curtain? The window was in the wrong place, though. Velda sat up, her eyes wide, as she demanded more from her cobwebbed mind than it was prepared to give. She had a sagging feeling inside, but she didn't know what or why. Her mouth was exceptionally dry. She felt across to her bedside table for a glass of water but there was no water and there was no table. Where was she?

Swinging her legs down to the floor, she silently crossed the room, moving towards the light. Yes, it was a curtain. She tugged it wide and was momentarily blinded by the brightness from outside.

The realisation of where she was and the cause of the sagging feeling inside slammed into her brain like a baseball bat. She was in one of the Jacklin guestrooms. God only knew how long she had been there. She remembered flashes of what had taken place, her thoughts having been filtered and sieved through the pall of strong barbiturates.

She was calm now, her thoughts as placid as a glassy lake. She knew what had to be done.

Velda strode over to the door and turned the handle. It was locked. They had locked her in, imprisoned her.

'Hello?' Velda shouted, knocking loudly. She repeated her call, ensuring that her voice sounded as normal as possible.

She heard movement outside the room.

'Hello? Can you open the door, please?'

It was Joseph who unlocked it. Concern and anxiety marked his face. 'Are you okay, Velda?'

She nodded. 'Sorry about earlier—but I know what we've got to do about her now—'

'Fight her!' Joseph interrupted. 'Get another attorney. Get a whole bunch of attorneys—she's not going to know what's hit her.'

'No,' Velda said quietly. She took his hand. 'Come and sit down here.' She led him to the bed and he sat beside her. 'What does Audrey want?'

Joseph shrugged. 'My money?'

'No, that's not it.'

'To make me look dumb?'

'Nope, that's not it either.'

'I don't know, Velda,' he answered impatiently. 'I give up—what *does* she want?'

'She wants a game,' she explained. 'It's as simple as that. She wants you to throw money at a whole bunch of attorneys and get whipped up in a big court battle but she doesn't really care if she wins or loses. Her whole life has been a game, a drama.'

'So, what? Do nothing—never divorce her?'

'Play the game back. Do what she would least expect.'

'And that is what exactly?' Joseph asked.

'Leave town. You and me. Pack up and go. We tell *nobody* where we're going—at least not for a while and we live someplace else, somewhere she can't find us.'

Joseph took her hand in his and met her gaze. 'You're serious, aren't you?'

Velda nodded.

'I'm guessing by that glint in your eyes that you've got some ideas of where you want to go?'

'Massachusetts—eventually.'

'Massachusetts? Jesus, Velda. Why not somewhere a little closer, like the moon?'

At that moment, Velda no longer needed a proposal. Her fanciful wedding ideas vanished. It was going to be just the two of them alone. A new state. A new start.

Chapter Fourteen

27th June 1976, Boston, Massachusetts, USA

It felt good to finally be able to tell someone everything. Every last detail that he had discovered. Last week he had escaped his parents' house with blood running from his nose and his ears echoing with his dad's brutal words. He had driven himself to the local hospital to be told that his nose was broken and there was nothing they could do to fix it. He had left the hospital and driven home, where he had found himself the main character in a fictitious story created by his dad. Jack, so the story went, had been attacked by masked assailants as he had left the school. His mom saw the story as factual and played the doting mother role to perfection. His dad's concern reached only to the moments when he was in the company of both his wife and son; the remainder of the time his and Jack's interactions were non-existent.

Today, after work, Jack couldn't face the prospect of another weekend at home. Having no destination in mind, he had driven across the Sagamore Bridge that linked the Cape to mainland Massachusetts. Route Six had flowed into Route Three. Signs for Boston had appeared and the idea of having someone to talk things over with had taken a hold, guiding him into the city.

'I just can't believe this,' Alice declared when he had finished his story. They had been sitting for some time, side by side, on her bed in her small dormitory. She stood up with her hands on her hips. 'Why would they fabricate an entire *life* like this? What are they hiding?'

Jack shrugged. 'Damned if I know.'

'But you're going to find out, right?' Alice asked. 'You must—you can't just leave it like this.'

'There's nothing more that can be done, Ali. Mr Chipman's friend has found all this out,' Jack said, pointing to the pile of paperwork on the floor in front of them, 'but he doesn't seem to think there's much more he can do.'

'There is one thing you can do,' Alice said.

Jack rolled his eyes. 'Try talking to them about it?'

'God, no. That obviously wouldn't work,' Alice cut in. 'No, I was going to say you could go to California. Find our grandparents and talk to them directly.'

For a long time, Jack stared at his sister. She was serious. The thought of visiting his grandparents had occurred to him the very moment that Mr Chipman had told him that they were still alive, but then, in all that had followed, his thoughts had been spun in a multitude of directions and, now that Alice presented the idea, it seemed the only logical thing to do. But of course, the reality of that decision was more easily said than done.

'I've got some money I can give you for the flight,' Alice said, intuiting one strand of his thoughts. 'You could go from here—get a flight out tomorrow.'

'Ali, be practical; I can't go tomorrow. I have a job, for one thing. And I can't just spring myself on them. Look, I'll write to them and see what happens—keep it simple and take it from there.'

Alice reluctantly agreed. 'I just can't believe it, Jack…'

'Nor would I, but the evidence is right there,' he said, pointing to the floor. 'The truth is this: our dad is two men; and we only know one of them.'

To add to Jack's list of ailments and injuries were a stiff neck and a painful lower back. He sat up from his awkward position in a sleeping bag on the floor beside Alice's bed. The thin curtains were doing a feeble job at holding back the streaming daylight. Alice's bed was empty. There was a note on it, addressed to him. *Gone to basketball. Write to our grandparents! Meet you back here for lunch. A xx* Underneath it was a notepad and pen.

Jack stretched, then winced at the stabbing pain from his ribs, still unable to believe that it was his own dad who had inflicted the injuries. He had always been a strict man, but he had never so much as laid a hand on Jack before. Were cracks beginning to appear in the previous, neatly sealed wall that had divided his dad's two lives? Had Jack caught a glimpse through the cracks to see the man that his dad really was?

He picked up the pen and paper and began to write. He knew from the first line that he wouldn't actually post it—not this version, at least. It contained everything—all his questions, all his feelings about his dad, all the details of his life so far. Everything. The finished letter ran to four pages. He signed his name at the bottom, then began to tear it up, peeling it apart, inch by inch. Then he wrote another letter to them, this one simple and short. *Dear George and Lucy, this letter might come as as much of a shock to you as the knowledge of your existence came to me. I am the second child of Roscoe (Joseph) and Velda Jacklin. I was born in 1956 in Hyannis*

Port, MA. *It is only recently that I came to learn that I had family on the other side of the country. I am hoping that you will write back and perhaps one day we might meet each other. Sincerely Yours, Harley Jacklin (Jack).*

He read the letter back. It was short and dour, but it said what it needed to say. If they were smart and read between the lines, they would understand that he had been lied to since birth and hopefully they would perceive the myriad of implications that came together with that revelation.

With the pen still poised in his hand, he decided to write another letter. *Dear Margaret, Well, my silent English friend, since my last letter things have gone from bad to worse. Friday I got into a terrible row with dad and we ended up yelling at each other. I blurted out what I knew about his past. He beat me real bad and I ended up in hospital. I've got a broken nose and I'm pretty bruised up. Margaret, I wish you would write me back—I could sure use your advice right now. Dad told Mom I got beat up at school, so she's being nice at the moment—I wonder whose side she would take, though, if she knew the truth... I don't know what to do next, now that I've blown the lid off it—Dad and I aren't even talking—he only speaks to me when Mom's around. I don't know how much more I can take of it. What should I do, Margaret? I wish I could just get on a plane and head back to you in Folkestone. Do you miss me at all? If you get this, Margaret, I sure would appreciate a response. Yours, Jack xx*

Jack looked at the letter and, for the first time, felt slightly foolish. What was he thinking? She clearly didn't want to have anything to do with him anymore. In his current frame of mind, he was half-tempted to shred the letter, just like the first one that he had written to his grandparents. But no, he decided that he would send it.

He looked at the clock: he still had a couple of hours before Alice would return. Placing the two letters on the bed, he climbed out of the sleeping bag and dressed. He used the bathroom, picked up the letters and left the dorm.

Having posted both the letters off, Jack crossed the city on the T line to Boston University Central, then strode across the open courtyard of Marsh Plaza, a nostalgic familiarity from his brief spell studying here guiding him to the correct building on the campus.

He bound up several flights of stairs until he reached Laura's bedroom. He knocked on the door and waited, unsure of exactly what he would say when—*if*—she answered.

Following a rattle of metal behind the door, it opened.

'Oh my God! What are you doing here?' Laura asked, throwing her arms around him.

He held her tightly, not expecting such a warm welcome. She felt strangely good in his arms. 'Passing by, thought I'd call in, make sure you're working hard.'

Laura broke their embrace and frowned at him suspiciously. 'Wait. What happened to your nose?'

'Long story. Got time for a hot chocolate?'

'Absolutely. Wait there and I'll go get my purse.'

Laura led them to a new coffee shop that had sprung up on Commonwealth Avenue. They carried their drinks to a small table close to the window.

Jack watched her as she wound the spoon slowly around her mug. She had changed in some subtle way since she had left the Cape six months ago. It wasn't her appearance—she was wearing a pair of bell-bottomed jeans and a light-yellow top—both of which he had seen before. Something in her face was different. Maturity? A sparkle of confidence, perhaps?

She caught him staring and smiled. 'What?'

'Nothing,' Jack said, flushing with inexplicable embarrassment.

'Come on then, let's hear this long story. As long as it's finished before classes start again on Monday, that is.'

Jack took a sip of his drink then began to relay the whole story. Given Laura's reactions, akin to Alice's, her father had evidently told her nothing of his and his colleagues' discoveries. He told her about the letter that he had just posted to his grandparents in San Francisco, feeling a peculiar sense of guilt at not mentioning the letter that he had also sent to Margaret.

'And how's the job going? Is my dad a better employer than Rory McCoy?' Laura asked with a grin.

'You know what, he's been good to me,' Jack answered. 'Really good. You're lucky to have him as your dad.'

'I know. When I was younger I used to get embarrassed by him—he wasn't like my friends' dads.' She sipped her drink and smiled at him. 'I used to look at your dad and wish mine were more like him.'

'Really?'

'Yeah. A normal job, a normal car, a normal house. Just, *normal*, you know? But now I love my dad's eccentricities.'

'Funny,' Jack began, 'I would have called my dad normal too, but he's anything *but* that...I just don't know him, Laura. Who is this local businessman war-hero that raised me? Is he even a good man?'

Laura leant over and placed her hand on his. 'You'll find out—I know you will.'

Jack curled his fingers into hers, enjoying the warmth of her grasp. 'Anyway, let's talk about something else. How are you getting on here? When are you coming back? The semester ended ages ago and you're still attending classes?' Jack sat back and listened to Laura. The husk of shyness had gone and she now spoke with a soft self-assurance.

An hour later, it was time for Jack to leave. He walked Laura back to her room.

'Well, thanks for dropping in, Jack—it was so lovely to see you.'

'You too,' he said. 'Let me know as soon as you return to the Cape.'

'I will. Take care with all your investigations, won't you?' she said, gently caressing his upper arms. She leant up and pecked him on the lips.

The kiss lingered and he felt a stirring inside that he had not felt since his visit to England two years ago. He saw Margaret's sweet face in the darkness of his closed eyes and pulled away. 'Bye,' he blurted, turning on his heels and heading back down the stairs.

Chapter Fifteen

24th August 2016, Chatham, Massachusetts, USA

'Can we just stay here forever? Would anyone *really* notice if we didn't go home?' Juliette asked with a yawn. She was lying in her bikini on Chatham Lighthouse Beach, a large floppy straw hat covering her face. The beach was packed with holidaymakers enjoying the cloudless sky.

Morton was sitting on his towel beside her with his shirt off, scooping up handfuls of hot sand and watching as it poured through the cracks between his fingers. He actually gave serious consideration to her question, imagining a new life in America. They would have to start all over again. He would have to establish himself here as a forensic genealogist. Back at home he had gained a reputation as someone who tackled complicated cases, which often brought him into contact with people on the wrong side of the law. Living here would certainly give him the one thing that he really needed right now: time. They had just three days left until they were due to fly from Boston to New York for the remainder of their honeymoon—the distinctly *non*-genealogical aspect. Then it was back to England. Back to a new genealogy case. 'Maybe,' he answered finally, with a large exhale.

'Maybe what?' Juliette muttered.

'Maybe we could up sticks and move here.'

'I was joking. Of course we can't move here.'

He picked up today's edition of the *Cape Cod Times*. His request—embellished and dramatised—had been published on page four under the melodramatic headline *The Missing Man*. The byline gave the writer's name as Hal Adelman, who had taken it upon himself to rummage in the newspaper's archives to include details of the original story that they had run back in December 1976. Hal had even included a photograph of the house on fire. Well, it would certainly get noticed more than the discreet couple of lines that he had been expecting to find. For the fourth or fifth time, Morton checked that the contact number in the story was correct. He pulled out his mobile phone to make sure that it was still switched on and not in silent mode, then he opened his bag and pulled out all the paperwork that he had generated during this trip so far. Once again, he went through the notes that he had made at his Aunt Alice's house. Laura Chipman's name was underlined.

He had spent a good deal of time trying to track down her whereabouts in Alberta, but still had no positive leads. He had tried various forms of social media and had sent several messages and emails to potential matches. But, as yet, nothing.

Turning to the next piece of research, he re-read the account of his grandfather's act of heroism in Korea. He was thinking it increasingly likely that the war had indeed provided him with a moment of epiphany—some awakening inside of a desire to be with Velda Henderson and not his wife and child. But it just didn't feel quite right. People abandoned their kids all the time, but Morton just couldn't imagine it of the man that he had seen in the photo album at Alice's house. He seemed so doting and caring of his two children. Maybe Morton struggled to imagine him abandoning his first child because he saw something of himself in his grandfather and it was an act completely unconscionable to him.

He scrutinised the date of the report of his grandfather's wartime deeds: November 1st, 1950. Then, one month later he had filed for divorce. The baby, Florence, had been born in 1951. But when, exactly? Morton couldn't find the answer amongst his paperwork. Logging into Ancestry on his mobile phone, he accessed the California Birth Index 1905-1995 and found the entry.

Name: Florence Jacklin
Birth Date: June 7, 1951
Gender: Female
Mother's Maiden Name: Fuller
Birth County: San Francisco

Morton remembered what Alice had said about her father—that he had been one of the first volunteers to enlist to fight in Korea. When did the conflict begin, exactly? He ran a quick Google search: 25th June 1950. Meaning that Joseph Jacklin was out of the country from June until November of that year. An online calculator estimated Florence Jacklin's conception to have been around the 14th September 1950.

'Joseph wasn't the father,' Morton said.

'What?' Juliette asked.

'The first baby—Florence—that might have been the reason he divorced Audrey. He returned home to find her pregnant and knew that there was no way the baby could be his. That would make your theory that he just upped and left his first wife and child behind much more plausible.'

'*Highly* likely, if you ask me,' Juliette commented from beneath her hat.

'Right, that's it,' Morton said, jumping up. 'Are you okay here, if I disappear off for a couple of hours?'

Juliette removed the hat from her face and frowned at him. 'Where are you going?'

'To pay another visit to my Aunt Alice—she's literally my only hope now. We leave in three days—and we know she knows more than she's letting on.'

Juliette nodded her agreement. 'Good idea—I'll be fine here until sunset. No rush. Good luck.'

He kissed her on the lips and strode across the beach towards the car.

MacMillan Pier was once again heaving. One of the whale-watching fleet had evidently just returned, its passengers jostling along the wooden jetty. Morton felt like a helpless fish trying to swim against the current, as he pushed through the crowds to get to *Alice's Art*.

The hut itself was swarming with prospective shoppers. Inside, he saw Jan looking flustered, taking money from one customer whilst answering a question from another. Now really wasn't going to be the best time to start pestering her. There was no sign of Alice.

He decided to wait until the crowds had abated. He walked over to the side of the pier and sat down, his legs dangling a few feet above the water. Below him, a shoal of small fish pinged about in seemingly random directions.

As he stared into the water, he felt for the first time since he had started searching that he might never get to meet his father. He thought of how his grandfather had so easily abandoned his first family and the idea was gaining traction in his mind that perhaps Alice was trying to spare his feelings, that his father simply didn't want to meet the child that he had unknowingly fathered more than forty years ago. It was a possibility to which he had previously given little thought. He had only really given consideration to two options: that his father was dead or alive. And, if the latter were true, that he would certainly want to meet Morton. This third option—that his father was alive but didn't want to know him—began to seep more deeply into his thoughts.

He turned to face the hut. The crowds had thinned somewhat—probably as much as they were going to do on a hot day in the middle of the high season. If Alice and Jan *were* trying to be kind to him, perhaps it was best to just walk away, so as not to upset things further.

He stood up and stared at the hut. Time passed as his thoughts lurched around in pendulum-like indecision. It would be so easy to walk away and just be grateful for what he had already learned on this trip. But he knew that the curiosity about his father's whereabouts would plague him to the grave; he couldn't leave without having tried everything, it just wasn't in him.

Morton crossed to the hut and found Jan handing a wrapped gift to a young woman.

'Well, hello again!' she beamed. 'What's this—one last tour of the Cape? Where's that lovely wife of yours?' she asked, craning her neck to look behind Morton.

'I've left her on a beach in Chatham,' he replied, trying to force a smile over his distinct lack of joviality.

'Oh, dear! Hope she didn't mind. And I'm afraid you've missed Ali—she's taken herself off to our shack up in the sand-dunes to paint.'

'Do you know when she's due back?' Morton asked, glancing at this watch. 'I was hoping to catch her before we left for New York.'

'Good question!' Jan answered, throwing her hands up in dismay. 'Maybe tomorrow, maybe next week. One time she went out there and stayed a whole month.'

'I don't suppose I can pay her a visit out there, can I?'

'That wouldn't go down too well.'

Morton exhaled sharply. This was his one final chance. 'Look, Jan, is there anything else you can tell me? I had the impression the other night that perhaps there was something that wasn't being said. I'm desperate to find him—*anything* at all you can give me to go on would be a help—even if, when I find him he just tells me to go away...'

Jan grimaced. 'Listen—I really want you to find your daddy, I really do, but I'm not the one that can help you. Alice has told you all she can—you've got her email so ask her any further questions you have. It's really not my place, Morton—I'm so sorry.'

He knew that he was putting her on the spot. She was uncomfortable. He wanted to say, 'Why do you have a photo of my dad in your house?' and 'Who is the woman with him?' but he just couldn't do it. It would be like someone asking him to divulge something that Juliette had expressly asked him not to. 'Okay,' he found himself saying. He smiled and pulled her into a hug. 'It was so lovely to meet you.'

'And you too.' She kissed him lightly on the cheek. 'We'll stay in touch—I promise.'

'That would be great. Bye,' Morton said, leaving the hut and joining the throng of people pushing their way towards Commercial Street.

He walked briskly with tears in his eyes, now completely certain that his father was out there but did not wish to meet him. Jan's words rang in his ears as he walked. '*…Alice has told you all she can…*' She wasn't allowed to say more.

His quest was all but over.

Chapter Sixteen

3rd April 1954, Barnstable, Massachusetts, USA

Velda was sitting back in the armchair with her eyes closed, listening to the last verse of Doris Day's *Secret Love*. She was wearing a pink felt poodle-skirt and had styled her short hair into fashionable curls. She wanted to look her absolute best for him when he got home.

'*...at last my heart's an open door and my secret love's no secret anymore,*' she sang along.

The song ended and the arm gently lifted the needle from the record, returning the house to its prior stillness. Velda opened her eyes and looked at the clock with a gasp. There was still so much left to do! What was she thinking?

She hurried into the kitchen and carefully pulled her apron over her hair. The room was large and modern—just like the rest of the house—containing white enamel cabinets, General Electric stove, dishwasher, washing machine and large refrigerator. They had purchased the house for $21,000 last year and it came with the latest in design and technology. It really was the most perfect home for them.

Opening the oven door, she checked on the cake—it looked and smelt amazing. She began to pour some icing sugar into a bowl when the doorbell sounded. Velda glanced at the clock again—no, it couldn't be him for another hour...unless he'd managed to finish early...and why was he ringing the bell?

She removed the apron and scuttled off to the front door. Just as she reached it, the bell rang again. She opened the door with a scowl.

An unfamiliar man—short, in a long brown mac with a briefcase—stood with a wide grin on his face. He removed his fedora hat. 'Good afternoon, Velda!' He took a step forwards, as if he were an old friend.

The visitor seemed surprised when Velda didn't move to permit him entrance. 'And who might you be?' she asked.

The man's face fell. 'Your husband didn't tell you I was coming over? It's me—Johnny Brucker...'

Velda stared blankly. Neither the face nor the name struck familiarity with her.

'Jeez, I know it's his twenty-sixth birthday and all that but, come on...what, he didn't say he'd asked Johnny Brucker over to talk about some investments he wants to make?'

Velda shook her head. 'Not a single word, Mr Brucker.'

'Well, is he home?' he asked, trying to look over Velda's shoulder.

'Not yet, no; he's at work.'

'I do apologise, Mrs Jacklin. I must have made an error,' he said, scratching his chin.

Velda watched as he stooped over and pulled something from his briefcase. A diary. He thumbed through it then stopped.

'No, no error. Here,' he said, passing the diary to Velda.

Roscoe Jacklin, 4pm (investments).

Mr Brucker looked at his wristwatch with a grimace. 'It's only a quick appointment—signing paperwork, mainly. I mean, I could come back…'

Velda retracted her outward irritation with the interruption, diverting it towards her husband. What was he thinking, making an appointment like this on his birthday? 'No, come on in. He must be almost home, if he made the appointment with you for four o'clock.'

Mr Brucker followed Velda into the kitchen.

'Please, take a seat. Can I get you a coffee?'

'Thank you—black, one sugar.'

As Velda made the man's drink, she was aware of a creeping sense of vulnerability. She turned frequently, not wanting her back to him. She stirred his coffee, standing at a peculiar angle that kept him in her peripheral vision. He was glancing around the room, taking everything in.

'Real nice place you've got here,' he commented.

'Thank you,' Velda said, hurrying the coffee to the table in front of him and wishing that Joseph would hurry up.

'Congratulations,' Mr Brucker said, 'If that's okay to say so.'

She presumed that he was referring to the house and mumbled her gratitude. Then she noticed that his head was bobbed and his raised eyebrows were pointing in the direction of her stomach. Had he guessed, or had Joseph told him? They had agreed not to tell anyone just yet… 'Early days,' Velda muttered. Where was Joseph?

Mr Brucker took a swig of the coffee, then placed his briefcase on the table, popped open the brass clasps and flipped the lid open. 'Listen, Mrs Jacklin. I can see you're real busy. Maybe you could help me fill some of these forms in—it's nothing financial or personal—just basic stuff.'

'Well, I guess that would be okay,' Velda replied uncertainly, eyes flicking to the front door.

Mr Brucker fumbled in his briefcase then withdrew a piece of paper and a pen. 'So, I take it given all the balloons and decorations, that I have his birthday of April 3rd 1928 correct?'

Velda nodded. 'That's right.'

'And where was he born, exactly?'

'Boston.'

'Okay,' Mr Brucker noted. 'And where and when was he lucky enough to make you his wife?'

'June sixth last year,' Velda answered. 'First Congregational Church, Wellfleet.'

Mr Brucker stroked his chin as he wrote. 'And you were Miss Velda Henderson—is that correct?'

The previous reassurance that this man clearly knew her husband now began to trouble her. She had absolutely no dealings in her husband's business and couldn't understand why knowing her maiden name was a necessity in his investment paperwork.

Finally, a key in the door!

Velda took a deep breath and was able to relax. 'We're in here!' she called quickly.

He strode into the kitchen with a smile.

'Joseph…I mean, Roscoe Joseph,' Velda stammered, 'your friend's here—about the investments.' But Velda knew instantly that something wasn't right. He was looking at the man with the same searching eyes that she herself had laid upon him.

Mr Brucker closed his briefcase, stood up and extended his hand towards Joseph. He wasn't offering his hand to shake, Velda realised, but handing him a small card of some sort.

Joseph took the card. 'Johnny Brucker. Private Investigator,' he read impassively.

A vacuum of silence ensnared the room as the true purpose of the visit crystallised.

'What does she want?' Joseph asked.

Mr Brucker smiled. 'To see you in court.'

Joseph laughed. 'On what charge, exactly?'

'Bigamy.'

'Now listen here, Johnny,' Joseph began, 'if you think that—'

'Don't bother,' Mr Brucker interjected. 'Your good wife here has confirmed everything. You married her last year while still married to Audrey. Court cases don't get much more open-and-shut than that, Joseph or Roscoe or whatever it is you're calling yourself now.'

'Get out of my house!' Joseph yelled.

Mr Brucker smiled, placed his fedora back on his head and picked up his briefcase. 'Good day to you folks.' He paused at the doorway and turned. 'Audrey said to say happy birthday. She wanted me to sing, but my voice ain't all that good.'

The slamming of the front door coincided with the smashing of the bowl containing the icing sugar. Velda screamed. 'That damned woman!' Velda exploded. 'When is she ever going to leave us alone?'

'Maybe never,' Joseph uttered solemnly. 'We've got a war on our hands, Velda. A real war.'

Chapter Seventeen

2nd October 1976, Hyannis Port, Massachusetts, USA

Jack was sitting at his desk in front of his bedroom window, watching and waiting for the storm to break. Thick clouds as black as coal were suspended no more than a hundred feet above the unbridled sea, as if awaiting a final command to assault the harbour and villages beyond. It was going to be a bad one, that much was certain. He was thankful that phase two of his job had ended just days before the first vestiges of winter had skulked in. The cemetery had been cleared and was now in the capable hands of a local maintenance company. All headstones had been cleaned and recorded and a map had been drawn of the cemetery, with each grave meticulously plotted. His work was now to bring life to the bones beneath the stones. On the desk behind him was a stack of books from the local library and an assortment of jumbled paperwork pertaining to the Sturgis headstones on which he was currently working—another notable local family after whom was named the library in Barnstable where Jack did much of his research.

A gust of wind shook the pine tree in the neighbour's garden, evicting an unhappy cardinal.

The storm was drawing closer.

From downstairs came a light banging sound. Jack raced to his bedroom door and down the stairs, meeting his mom at the bottom. They were both racing towards the wedge of mail protruding from the front door. Jack dived in front of her and snatched it from the mouth of the letterbox.

'Whatever's the matter with you?' his mom snapped.

Jack ignored her and quickly flicked through the stack of letters. 'I've just been waiting on some information for work,' he answered, pulling out a thin white envelope addressed to him. 'And here it is.'

She eyed him distrustfully but said nothing, reaching out and taking the rest of the mail.

Upstairs, Jack closed his bedroom door and sliced into the letter. It was post-marked California, the fourth letter from his paternal grandparents. His first letter to them, they had admitted in their initial response, had come as a complete surprise; they had claimed to know nothing at all of Jack and Alice. Even their whereabouts had come as a revelation. His reply had been lengthy. Set against a barrage of questions about them and their family in San Francisco, Jack had shared some information about Alice and him. Their response had come quickly, answering all of his questions in detail. Having bided his time, Jack then broached the thorny subject of his dad's early life. The reply had been revelatory. It had spoken of his childhood friendship with the girl next door—Velda Henderson—that had turned more serious as they had grown up. They had been uncertain as to the reasons, but Joseph and Velda had then split up and Joseph had gone on to marry Audrey Fuller in 1949 before signing up for service in Korea. He had been injured in the war, returning home in 1950, before one day taking off with Velda and never returning.

Jack pulled the latest letter from the envelope and began to read.

Our dear Jack, It was a great pleasure to receive your last letter. We were delighted to hear all about your summer and how the job at the cemetery is progressing. It sounds stimulating and challenging for you. Thank you, also, for your update on Alice and the drawing—she truly is a magnificent artist with a promising career ahead of her. We have had the picture professionally framed and it now has pride of place on the grand piano. You both are doing so very good. Your grandfather and I are both keeping well. We go to fitness classes once a week and play tennis regularly—not to mention our busy social life! There seems a never-ending stream of friends pouring through the door. To answer your question, Jack, yes, I do understand your need to know the past. While it is our greatest wish not to muddy the waters in any way, we won't lie to you. You ask about your father's first wife and details of the divorce. Her name was Audrey Fuller and they married in March 1949, here in San Francisco. I'm afraid to tell you this—there was no divorce. For various reasons, many of which we can only surmise, Audrey would not grant it to your dad. Audrey died in 1954 and the threatened court action against your dad never happened, thankfully. We repeat our open invitation to you and your sister to visit us. We would so dearly like to meet you both. With kind affection, Lucy & George

Jack stared at the letter, his eyes being drawn back to her name. *Audrey Fuller.* His dad was a bigamist. Regardless of the fact that Audrey had died, it didn't change the simple fact that his parents' marriage was illegal. And his mom was irrefutably complicit. It suddenly explained a lot: the reason for the complete dislocation of the past; the refusal to discuss his dad's family history; and the labyrinth of lies and deceptions that had evolved through the decades.

But what was he going to do with the information? He and Alice had discussed visiting their grandparents—possibly next spring break.

But what to tell their parents? They were already sitting on their own set of lies and deceptions...

Jack read the letter once more, then hid it with the others at the back of his work folder and tried to refocus his mind on the task in hand: compiling a biography on the Sturgis family. He sat at his desk and gazed outside. The great slabs of black in the sky had inched to the shoreline. Shards of rain began to slice into the lawn. It was the kind of hard rain that came as a precursor to an absolute deluge. Just a handful of seconds passed before the clouds ruptured and the house sounded as though it was under a machine gun attack.

His gaze dropped from the watery grey diffusion of the window down to his notebook. He read back what he had written about John Sturgis but the words had no impact against that with which his mind was contending: bigamy. The word was lodged, tumour-like, obstinately at the forefront of his thoughts, refusing to budge.

He would have to tell Alice straight away, there was no choice: this situation had made them promise never to keep secrets from one another.

'Aren't you hungry, Jack?' his mom asked across the table.

'Sorry—it was good but I'm full,' he replied, setting his knife and fork down beside the half-eaten chicken pie.

'Did you use an entire chicken?' his dad asked, turning and winking at Jack. He too placed his cutlery down with a sigh that said that the dinner had beaten him.

'Oh, stop it,' Velda said with a chuckle. 'I don't suppose you boys have any space for dessert, then?'

'Well, I expect we could squeeze a *little* in. Don't you think so, Jack?'

Jack nodded, his mask—replete with broad, beaming smile—safely in place. Every meal time, or other occasion that necessitated that the three of them be in the same room at the same time was identical: a bizarre and nightmarish game where, by tacit agreement, they played versions of themselves without pasts.

Velda grinned as she collected the dinner plates from the table.

A crash of thunder from close by coincided almost perfectly with the peal of the doorbell, causing the three of them to pause and consider if they had heard correctly.

'I'll go,' Jack volunteered, leaping up, grateful for an excuse to leave the table. As he headed to the door, he heard his dad commenting that it was probably one of the neighbours needing something because of the storm. But it wasn't, it was Laura. She was standing under the cover of the porch, her saturated hair stuck to the side of face and water dripping from her coat. 'Hey. You sure picked a good time to come here.' Jack stepped to one side. 'Come on in.'

'Didn't I just,' she replied, stepping inside the house.

He kissed her lingeringly on the lips. It was still new and slightly awkward; they had grown closer and crossed the line of friendship into a new territory, unfamiliar to him. Nobody but the two of them and Michael knew about it and it had yet to receive any official designation. Dating. The word was exotic-sounding to him and came with such expectations.

'Are your mom and dad in?' she mouthed silently, to which Jack nodded. She rolled her eyes.

'Who is it, Jack?' his dad called.

'Just Laura—we're going up to my room.'

'Oh, but don't you want any dessert?' his mom called from the kitchen. 'There's enough for Laura, too.'

Jack raised his eyebrows questioningly to Laura. She shook her head. 'No, we're okay, thanks.'

In his bedroom, Jack closed the door, grateful to have been saved from the charade downstairs.

'Just Laura?' she chided, backing him playfully into the door. 'Just Laura?'

'Yeah, just Laura,' he joked. Jack smiled and pulled her close. He kissed her again, but this time the awkwardness had vanished and passion had taken hold.

Chapter Eighteen

27th August 2016, Boston Logan International Airport, Massachusetts, USA

Morton's head was killing him and he was struggling to keep up. Juliette was marching a few paces ahead of him, dragging her suitcase behind her. Every tiny sound in the busy airport car park was amplified, smashing against his eardrum. The migraine's arrival this morning—probably his worst ever and the first since leaving England—was no coincidence, for today was the day that they were leaving Massachusetts, thereby ending the active search for his father.

'Oh, air con—thank God,' Morton mumbled, as they entered the terminal building. 'Can we stop for a second?'

Juliette paused and turned. 'Tablets not kicking in yet?'

'No,' he breathed, gently wiping sweat from his brow. After a long, slow inhalation he said, 'Come on, then, lead the way to check-in.'

'Listen, we've got bags of time—let's get a water and have a sit down first,' Juliette said.

'Or a coffee?' he suggested through squinted eyes.

'No, a water. Go and sit over there—' she directed him to a cluster of plastic seats, '—and I'll get us a drink.'

He sat down, only too willing to accept Juliette's orders, and held his head in his hands. He looked and felt pitiful. On the journey here Juliette had tried to console him and frame the failure to find his father in a different way. 'Look at all that you *have* discovered,' she had said with great enthusiasm. 'You've found your dad's high school year book, which included his photo; you found the report into your grandfather's death, which included *his* photo; you've been to their house; you've met your grandmother; you've met your aunt *and*, best of all, you've had a glorious two weeks of honeymoon with me—with another week in New York still to come. I'd say that was pretty good going.'

Morton had managed a smile, realising that he was coming across as being ungrateful. He had realised, too, upon hearing his achievements listed in such a way, that he had accomplished an awful lot in a short time. But it felt as though he had run a marathon and stopped just a few yards from the finish line.

'Leaving Massachusetts doesn't mean the search is over,' Juliette had continued. 'You might still get a phone call from the article—not everyone reads the paper the day it comes out, you know.'

Not a single person had yet contacted him about the story in the newspaper. Not one. It was like a giant conspiracy, Morton had thought, recalling the pages and pages of classmates that had attended Barnstable High School with his father. Not one of them, apparently, still resided on Cape Cod or read the local paper.

'Besides which,' Juliette had added. 'There must still be some research you can do back home: this can't be the one and only genealogical case that Morton Farrier abandons without completing.'

She was right, of course. And he had already begun working on his next steps: to trace each and every one of his father's classmates. He wouldn't give up until he had found him, even if he didn't wish to be found; he had to hear those words from the man himself.

In the darkness of his mind, his thoughts continued to mull over his research. Had he done everything he could? At least, given that he was on honeymoon, had he done *enough*?

'Here, I got you a water,' Juliette said, hauling him back to the present moment. 'And I found this for you, too.'

Morton held out his hand and took the water. With his eyes half-shut, he glanced up to her other hand. Nothing. Then, he saw the figure standing beside her.

It was him.

Chapter Nineteen

24th December 1976, Hyannis Port, Massachusetts, USA

Velda opened her wardrobe door and admired the impressive stack of Christmas presents. Boxes and packages of various sizes. *And such beautifully decorative wrapping! They look like something out of the window display in Woolworth's,* she thought, as she bent down to pick them up. It was the same routine each year—they had an evening meal together, then Velda would arrange the presents neatly under the tree in the sitting room where they would sit together and play board games—Monopoly was the usual favourite—until bedtime. She smiled at the recollection of countless past Christmases, all now smudged together into one warm memory. *How quickly time has passed,* she lamented. Memories of her own childhood Christmases back in San Francisco were sketchy and thin. She could see herself and Beatrice opening presents, laughing, singing and eating. Yet the memory of her mother was inanimate—almost like a hidden part of Velda's mind was projecting a static mental image of her. Velda could see her now—sitting in her favourite spot, not moving, not joining in the gaiety that surrounded her, not even blinking. Velda had no memories at all to call upon of her dad at Christmas, a sad notion that repeated itself at some point every holiday season.

She pulled herself back from her memories and continued carefully selecting gifts from the wardrobe. With a small pile in her arms—she didn't want to crush the delicate bows and ribbons—Velda headed out of the room to the stairs. She paused outside Alice's bedroom. She could hear low whispers between Jack and her—too quiet even to catch the gist of their conversation. She could take a good guess, though. Jack had gotten into yet another fight with his dad about the past.

Velda continued down the stairs with her pile of presents, wondering where all this friction was going to end up. The secrets of their past were returning. For the last few months they had been wondering where Jack had been getting his information from—then yesterday Roscoe had taken delivery of the mail and had seen a letter addressed to Jack, postmarked in San Francisco.

Had they done the right thing? Velda wondered, as she set the presents down in front of the tree. They had talked endlessly about what to do with the letter. It was Velda, in the end, who took the decision to steam it open and read the contents out loud to her bewildered husband. By the end of the letter, Velda's voice was quivering. It was from George and Lucy—evidently part of ongoing correspondence—and made explicit the details of what had happened to Audrey and her baby. She had stood staring at Roscoe, completely aghast. Neither of them had spoken for several minutes.

'We always knew the day might come,' Roscoe had finally said.

'Yes,' Velda had agreed absentmindedly. But, actually, she hadn't thought that the day would ever come; she thought their meticulous reconstruction of the past had worked. Maybe they had been too defensive in their handling of Jack's curiosity about the family. In hindsight, it was inevitable that a kid like him would find a way to the truth. *Always inquisitive, that boy...*

'Now what do we do?' Velda had stammered.

Roscoe had shrugged. 'It's over—one way or another.'

In their haze of shock, they had failed to hear Jack entering the room. He had seen the open envelope beside the kettle, snatched the letter from his mother, then had hastily read it.

Velda pulled herself back to the present and blinked away the tears in her eyes that ran from the memory of the ensuing argument. Neither Jack nor Roscoe had handled it well—both of them were as fiery and stubborn as the other. Negotiating between the two of them, they had agreed with her to discuss the situation after a normal Christmas. And that's just what they were going to have.

'What a lovely tree,' Velda whispered to herself, painting on a false smile, and forcing the recent trouble to the back of her mind. It was a Nova Scotia Balsam, a fine-looking specimen that she had covered with tinsel, baubles and lights. With the presents underneath, it looked just perfect—possibly the best one that she could remember.

Switching off the main house lights, she selected a Christmas album, placed it on the record player, took a deep breath and closed her eyes to steady her mind.

Moments later she reopened her eyes and looked at the clock. Six forty-five. Just enough time to squeeze in a few games before bed. 'Where's he gone?' she muttered, shifting the boxes of Christmas chocolates to the end of the table, giving them space to play.

'Roscoe? Hurry up!' she called, doubting that her voice would have carried down to the basement. She moved to the top of the stairs. The light was still on down there—goodness only knew what he was doing. 'Roscoe! Would you hurry up—we're almost ready to play.'

She sighed as she waited, then she called out again. 'Roscoe Jacklin—are you down there?'

Rolling her eyes, she descended into the basement, mumbling her annoyance at her husband. 'Roscoe, I've been—'

Her words faltered at the sight. Her heart tripped up and her legs weakened. She reached out and grabbed the newel post to stop herself from collapsing. Her mind began to shut down and her breathing became shallow, rasping.

She wanted to shout his name, call for help, but she barely had enough air to breathe.

Painfully slowly, she edged her way closer to him, all the while struggling to pull oxygen in and out of her aching body.

She stopped and looked at him. He was floating in mid-air, his black shoes—impeccably shiny—a good three feet off the ground. A high-backed chair was lying on the floor behind him. His face was an odd shade of purple, like a grape. His eyes looked swollen and bulbous. A pocket of chin fat was squished between his lower jaw and the thick sausage of rope that was wrapped around his neck.

She took his left hand in hers —crimson and tepid—and a strange calmness filtered through her—as if flowing from her husband's lifeless body. 'Oh, Roscoe,' she sobbed. Why hadn't she seen this coming? It was Jack's fault—that much was absolutely certain. He had somehow managed to break through the invisible wall to the past that she and Roscoe had put up twenty-six years ago when they had fled California, leaving their old lives behind. She thought back over the long road that had taken them from California to Massachusetts. It had begun with four months of acute nervousness in a small town in Kansas, where they had barely left their rented accommodation. Then had followed seven months in a godforsaken town in Ohio, where they had begun tentatively to engage in a normal life. But caution had moved them on to a spell in Pennsylvania. There, they had lived an anonymous city life, slipping in and, ten months later, back out unnoticed. It was upon reaching Massachusetts that Joseph had finally relaxed into his new name of Roscoe and the past was no longer discussed nor feared. Even the wedding had proceeded with ignorance of the past; it wasn't bigamy because they were different people. Audrey's name was never mentioned again until that damned private investigator had tracked them down. But that had been dealt with and their lives had continued. Until now. Until Jack had taken it upon himself to ruin everything.

Velda squeezed her husband's hand and vowed to keep what remained of the truth hidden; she knew what she had to do next.

Letting his hand drop into a gentle sway, she turned to face the bank of tools fixed to one wall. Crowbars. Hammers. Screw-drivers. Pliers. Every type of washer, nail and screw known to man. Saws. Velda reached up and lifted one of the bright steel blades down from its hooks. Standing on the chair behind him, she sunk the saw's razor-like teeth into the rope and began to cut.

With each forward motion of the saw, Roscoe's limp body swayed—an unnatural and gruesome ethereal dance.

Velda persisted without pause until Roscoe wilted to the floor like a released marionette puppet.

She unwrapped the rope from around his neck and tossed it to one side. She kissed his cool cheek, then headed for the stairs. Taking one final glance back, she switched off the light, pulled the door closed and made her way back upstairs. As she crossed to the kitchen, she was greeted by the opening bars of Bing Crosby singing *Silent Night*.

Velda opened one of the cupboards, her eyes scanning among the bowls and saucepans in front of her. There! She found what she was looking for—a large jug, which she proceeded to fill under the tap.

Water lapped at the edges of the jug as she walked, tiny puddles on the floor demarking her path into the sitting room.

The clock in the hallway struck seven.

'...*Sleep in heavenly peace*...' Velda found herself singing along, as she began to liberally douse the baseboard of the Christmas tree until the electrics began to fizz. '...*Sleep in heavenly peace*...'

Something clicked at the bottom of the tree, followed by a hissing that sounded like a Catherine wheel firework in full spin, making Velda jump back.

Then, flames. Small, smokeless and inquisitive, they reached up and nibbled at the edge of one of the Christmas presents. A camera for Roscoe, if Velda remembered correctly. The flames became more daring and wrapped themselves around the gift, licking up to the one sitting above it.

Velda felt an increasing warmth at her feet, as the flames touched the base of the tree, momentarily shrivelling the needles into black spikes before reducing them to nothing.

The heat pushed Velda a few paces back. The whole tree was now alight and smoke began to curl across the ceiling. All the presents were burning. The flames were now just inches from the thick curtains.

Humming along to the final bars of *Silent Night*, Velda turned and left the living room, closing the door behind her, then made her way up to her bedroom. As she passed Alice's room, she could hear them still talking—more loudly this time. Their voices were energised, happy.

Sitting on her bed, she waited.

It took four minutes before the record player gave up playing Christmas songs.

Another five minutes until the sounds of the fire tearing through the ground floor reached her ears. Snapping, breaking and devouring. The stench of smoke began to get stronger and more acrid.

It was time.

Velda stood up and entered the hallway. The fire had reached the front door and was stretching long red fingers through the banister rails.

She screamed loudly. 'Alice! Jack!' Another scream and Alice's bedroom door flew open.

'What?' Alice began, before the raging inferno at the bottom of the stairs caught her attention.

'We've got to get out—quick!' Velda shouted.

'Where's Dad?' Alice screamed.

'I don't know!' Velda cried. 'I need to call the fire department,' she said, running into her bedroom.

'Mom, there's no time!' Jack shouted, reaching out and grabbing her wrist. 'We've got to get out.'

'Jack's window!' Alice blurted. 'We can climb out onto the porch roof.'

At that moment, the house's wiring went, taking away the light. In a muddle of darkness, they ran into Jack's bedroom. He pulled up the window, bringing a gust of wintry wind into the room.

'Come on, Mom!' he directed, guiding her towards the opening.

Velda pulled herself up onto the ledge and crawled out onto the snow-covered shingles above the porch. On hands and knees, she slowly dragged herself along the edge.

'Go to the end, then hang down,' Jack ordered from behind her. 'Then go next door and get help.'

Velda reached the end and turned to lower herself down. She looked back at the window. Jack was out, but Alice had vanished.

Before she could speak, her freezing fingers slipped from the roof, sending her falling backwards into a bush below. 'Where's Alice?' she screamed, managing to stand up. 'Where's Alice?'

'Gone back in to get Dad,' Jack yelled. 'Hurry and get help!'

Velda was numb. The blanket over her shoulders, now heavy from the falling snow, did nothing to stop the acute quivering that rattled through her body. The police tape barricade, vibrating in the icy wind against her hands, had confined her to the street. The swelling congregation behind her—a motley mixture of prying and anxious neighbours and the whole gamut of emergency service personnel—were rendered faceless by the darkness of the night.

Velda's eyes followed the thick snakes of white hose that crossed her lawn from the hydrant, into the hands of the firefighters, who were battling the great rasping flames that projected from every window of the house. *Her* house.

One of the firefighters—the chief, she assumed—approached her. He was sweating and his face was marked with black blotches. 'Ma'am—are you *sure* your husband and daughter are still inside?'

'Yes,' she heard herself say.

'They couldn't have slipped out to get something from the grocery store or...?'

'No,' Velda sobbed. 'They're inside. Please find them.'

The fire chief nodded and turned back towards the house.

A moment later, without fanfare or warning, the house collapsed. The shocked gasps of her neighbours and the stricken cries of the firefighters on the lawn were lost to the appalling cacophony of metal, brick, wood and glass crumbling together, crescendo-ing into the night sky. A funnel of dense black smoke, peppered with flecks of bright red and orange, clashed in mid-air with the flurrying of falling snow.

Then, an odd stillness.

That her house—her *home*—could be reduced to this pile of indescribable burning debris in front of her shocked her anew.

This wasn't how it was supposed to be.

The hermetic seal that had neatly separated past and present had just ruptured spectacularly.

And now it was all over.

Somebody touched her shoulder and said something. She turned. It was her son, Jack. Either Velda's ears were still ringing with the sound of the house disintegrating, or Jack was speaking soundlessly. There was an urgency to his voice.

Velda tried to reply but a sagging sensation in her heart emanated out under her skin and down into her quivering limbs. Her legs buckled from beneath her and she crumpled helplessly into the snow.

She could hear her name being called. She was cold—so terribly cold—and couldn't move. She opened her eyes and saw Jack. Then she remembered that she had seen him before everything went black. The awfulness of the evening struck her memory with a force that made her gasp and sit up for breath.

'Alice,' Velda managed to say. 'Where is she?'

'They've just taken her to the hospital,' Jack answered, pointing to an ambulance departing with lights flashing and sirens blaring. 'She'll be okay…but…they haven't found Dad yet.'

She turned towards the house—or what was left of it. It was still blazing. 'Look what you've done…' she breathed.

'Pardon me?' Jack said. 'What did I do?'

Her grey eyes were cutting as she spoke. 'It's all your fault, Jack.'

'You know who probably did this?' Jack seethed quietly, pushing his face just inches from hers. 'Dad—that's who. Just like he did with his first wife and kid… Yeah, you think I'm stupid or something? Dad suddenly looks set for jail for bigamy, then they get killed in a fire with mysterious circumstances.'

Velda held his gaze the whole time he spoke. She had never seen him so angry.

'I know everything, Mom.'

Velda spoke softly. 'You've ruined everything, Jack. Why couldn't you just leave things alone?'

'I can't believe you're being serious. After all the lies you've told us… it's you and Dad who're to blame, Mom.'

'Just go, Jack. Just go. Leave.'

'Fine. But I'm never coming back.'

Chapter Twenty

30th December 1976, Hyannis Port, Massachusetts, USA

Jack was sitting on the edge of the bed, a notepad resting on his knees. A pen was poised in his hand but he was struggling to put all that had happened into words. So far, he had written the date—the only thing that he was certain of right now. Should he tell Margaret all that had occurred in the last few days? About all the family secrets? About the fire? Should he tell her about his growing relationship with Laura? It felt wrong, somehow, to maintain a connection to Margaret since he and Laura were now officially dating. Despite her not answering his letters, he still felt something for Margaret—like he owed her one more letter, an explanation of sorts. This would be the last one, he decided. A final goodbye. It fitted with the rest of his life and the closing down of the past. Only he, unlike his father, would not pretend that the past had never existed.

'Okay,' Jack muttered, putting pen to paper. *Dear Margaret, This is probably the last time you'll hear from me. Dad's dead. There was a big fire on Christmas Eve—our place is now a pile of ash and Mom and my sister are living with a neighbor. They blame me, so I'm staying with a friend from college. He's lending me everything—I have nothing left. The truth is out, it's all over. I don't know what to do. Except I need to leave town. I hope you have a good life, Margaret and maybe one day we'll meet again. Yours, Jack xx*

Jack folded the letter into an envelope and tucked it into the rucksack that was packed and waiting by his feet. Pretty well everything that he owned now fitted into that one bag.

Taking a final, lingering look around the room that he had called his bedroom for the past week, Jack stood up, picked up the rucksack and made for the door. He picked up his only other possession, the box containing his grandfather's war memorabilia, and slowly descended the stairs. A waft of cooking smells—coffee and bacon, he thought, drifted up to greet him.

Downstairs, he entered the kitchen. The conversation taking place at the table stopped and Mr Chipman, Michael and Laura all looked at him. He saw the same pity in their eyes as he had seen there every day since the fire.

Laura smiled. 'Do you want some breakfast before we go?'

'No, I'll be okay—I'll get something at the station,' Jack replied.

'Are you sure you want to go, Jack?' Mr Chipman asked. 'You know you're welcome to stay here for as long as you need.'

'I know that, Mr Chipman, and thank you very much, but this is something I need to do.'

'I understand, son.'

Michael cleared his throat. 'The funeral is on the eighth of January…'

Jack nodded. 'Alice said. I won't be going, though.'

A long silence lingered in the room before Laura spoke. 'Okay, do you want to get going?'

'Yeah, I think so—don't want to miss my bus.'

Mr Chipman and Michael rose from their chairs, meeting Jack part way across the kitchen. Michael pulled Jack into an embrace. 'You take care out there. I'll be over to see you in the next break.'

Jack held his best friend tightly, not wanting to let him go. He knew that he would never return to Cape Cod and only hoped that Michael was good to his word and came to see him. He broke away and moved into Mr Chipman's outstretched arms.

'It's been real good having you around, Jack. It's been a pleasure working with you and if you ever change your mind—your job will always be here. I mean that.'

'Thank you.'

'Same goes for your bedroom—it'll always be here for you.'

'I really appreciate everything you've done for me, Mr Chipman—really.'

'Okay, enough of all this,' Laura said, reaching for Jack's hand. 'Let's get going.'

Mr Chipman and Michael stood on the porch and waved as Jack climbed into Laura's car.

Laura turned to him with a smile, as she pulled out from the driveway. 'You're sure about this?'

'Absolutely. Let's go.'

'And you don't want to swing by to see Alice or—'

'No,' Jack interjected, as they drove past the end of Iyanough Avenue. His former home—still enclosed within a weave of police tape—had been reduced to an unsightly pile of unidentifiable rubble. His car, standing beside the house, had been damaged beyond repair. According to Alice, the fire department had managed to pull out a few bits and pieces, but nothing of his. She was still in hospital, suffering from first-degree burns and lacerations to her arms. With the fire raging, she had re-entered the house and had checked all the upstairs rooms for their dad. Then, she had somehow managed to drop down over the banisters to search their dad's study. It had been there that she had almost succumbed to the smoke, before being rescued by firefighters and pulled out of the window moments before the house had collapsed. 'He has to have been in the basement,' she had said afterwards. And she had been right; his body—burned and crushed beyond all recognition—had been retrieved from the basement two days ago. An accident—that was where the investigation was so far pointing—possibly originating with the Christmas tree. But Jack knew better—he was certain that it had been started deliberately by their dad: the bigamist's final act of cowardice, a sardonic ending for the lauded war veteran.

As they drove along Main Street, Jack's eyes were drawn to Rory's Store. He craned his neck as they drove past. The old man was standing outside, hands on his hips chatting to a customer—moaning, likely. Jack grinned. It was almost a year ago that he had stopped working there. So much had happened in the intervening months; he was a different person now, about to embark on a new life, leaving this one in Massachusetts behind.

With an ironic smirk, he realised that what he was about to do was the exact reverse of what his dad had done in 1950.

'What are you smiling at?' Laura asked.

Jack took a long breath as they entered the Mid-Cape Highway. 'Just day-dreaming about life in San Francisco.'

'It's a big step, alright,' Laura commented.

She was right: it was a massive step into the unknown. In an emotional phone call two days after the fire, he had spoken to his grandparents for the first time in his life. He was going to live with them, in the house in Cow Hollow in which his father had grown up. He planned to go back to college. And Laura, Michael and Alice had promised to come out to stay in the spring break.

They entered the Sagamore Bridge, leaving the Cape behind them. In front, was his future. 'I'm ready.'

Chapter Twenty-One

27th August 2016, Boston Logan International Airport, Massachusetts, USA

Morton stared at him, dumbfounded. His thoughts were stuck behind the mulish spikes that were piercing his brain, refusing to make sense of the situation. He looked to Juliette for explanation. She'd found him? Juliette's expression and her casual shrug suggested otherwise. A coincidence? Definitely not.

'Hi,' he said.

'Hi,' Morton replied, slowly standing. He looked again at Juliette for guidance. He'd spent so long thinking about the search for his father that he hadn't stopped to consider what he might say or do if they were ever to meet. And yet, here he was. He looked very much like the photograph that Juliette had surreptitiously taken at his Aunt Alice's house; his youthful face belied his sixty years. He was precisely Morton's height, his dark hair having the odd smattering of grey. His chestnut brown eyes were warm and welcoming, but still Morton couldn't speak.

'The Missing Man,' Juliette quipped. 'Found, wandering Boston airport.'

In perfectly mirrored synchronisation, the two men opened their arms and stepped into an embrace.

Morton held him like he had held no other, as tears rushed uncontrollably down his cheeks. The long journey that had started when he was just sixteen years old, when his father had blurted out that he had been adopted, was over. His fastidiousness, his stubbornness, his forensic genealogy, had been rewarded.

Time passed, but he hadn't a clue how much. He held on to his father and continued to sob wet puddles into his grey t-shirt.

Morton eventually let him go and took a step back, taking the proffered tissue from Juliette. 'What...? Where did you come from?' he managed to say.

'I just flew in from Canada,' he answered, dabbing his eyes.

'But how did you know?' Morton asked, breathlessly. 'I can't believe it...'

'Neither can I,' he laughed.

'How?' Morton muttered.

'My sister. She told me everything after you stopped by her house the other night. I don't think she believed you when you first contacted her, then when you showed up, she knew. She told me, then ran off to bury her head in the sand dunes. I must say, I was pretty shocked.'

'You had no idea that Margaret had had a baby?' Juliette asked.

He shook his head. 'None at all. I wrote her a whole bunch of letters but she never replied.'

'She...she never got them,' Morton muttered through his sniffles. 'Someone—her dad, I assume—intercepted them. Sorry, but I opened them.'

Jack nodded and smiled. 'So my sister said—I don't blame you—I would've done the same thing in your position.' Jack looked at his watch. 'How long do you guys have?'

'Only about half an hour,' Juliette said with a grimace.

'How about we try and cram in as much of the past forty years as we can?'

Morton nodded, still trying to convince his brain to push past the combined barrier of pain and shock. 'Less than a minute per year,' Juliette laughed. 'Good luck with that.'

'I can't believe it...' Morton repeated, needing to sit back down. 'I just can't believe you're here.'

'You wouldn't believe the hours of research he's put in to finding you,' Juliette said.

Jack smiled, sitting beside Morton and placing his hand on his leg. 'Jeez—I hope I'm worth it—that's a lot to live up to.'

Morton continued to stare at him, stunned. The man beside him, in so many ways a stranger, was paradoxically so familiar. It felt to him more like meeting up with a best friend after several years' absence than the very first time that they had ever clapped eyes on one another.

'So, let me see if I understand things correctly,' Jack began. 'Margaret was forced to give you up. Her brother and his wife couldn't have kids and they adopted you? Is that right?'

'Yes...' he stuttered, '...that's right.'

'Is Margaret...is she still alive?'

'Yes, alive and well. She lives in Cornwall. She's married with two daughters. Happy.'

'That's good to hear. I often think of her and wonder what happened to her. I've got something you might like to see,' he said, reaching into the back pocket of his jeans. 'Here.'

It was a photograph needing no explanation. It was Jack and Margaret standing together outside the Farrier household on Canterbury Road, Folkestone. His biological mother and father together. They were leaning on each other, smiling, their fingers interwoven. 'Wow,' was all that Morton could muster.

'It's the original—I'd like you to have it.'

'Are you sure?'

'Absolutely—I've made a copy for myself. It just seems right that you have it,' Jack said, patting Morton's leg.

'Thank you.'

Jack laughed. 'I don't mean to get too base, but that was my last day in England; you were in that photo, too.'

Morton laughed. 'Saturday the fifth of January,' he stated, recalling the exact dates of their visit from his research.

'If you say so, then, yeah,' Jack laughed. 'I still can't believe this. When Alice told me I thought she was kidding. Then she went on and on with so much detail I knew that it wasn't a joke. My God—a son I never knew…I don't know…it's just unbelievable…so, tell me about yourself.'

Something—the pills or the shock, he didn't know which—released the talons from inside his head; he could think again. He was aware that time was running painfully low and he had his own questions to ask, so he kept it brief, condensing great chunks of his life into small portions. He sped through his childhood, college and university, an overview of his career in forensic genealogy, and ended with meeting and marrying Juliette.

'You've done very well for yourself,' Jack commented at the end. 'I'm real glad to know that you're settled and happy.' He looked at his watch. 'And I guess you want to know a bit about me?'

'As much as you can say in thirteen minutes,' Morton encouraged.

'Okay. So, after the fire on Christmas Eve seventy-six, I took off to stay with my grandparents in San Francisco. I stayed there a few years—ironically in my dad's old bedroom—anyway, I went to college and studied forensic archaeology. I married a lovely lady from back home, Laura and we—'

The penny dropped—he knew why there had been a hint of recognition of the woman in the photograph that Juliette had discovered at Alice and Jan's house—Morton had seen her in the *Barnacle* year book. 'Laura Chipman?' Morton interrupted.

'Yeah, that's her,' Jack said with a look of surprise. 'You know her?'

'I just stumbled upon her in the course of my research.'

'Oh, I see,' he laughed. 'Yeah, she's amazing. We've got one son, George—named for my grandad.'

He had a brother...The revelations were coming thick and fast—too fast for his mind to keep up. Rafts of questions kept springing up, before being replaced, unanswered with another.

'I'm now a professor, teaching forensic archaeology and Laura is an obstetrician.'

'Forensic archaeology?' Juliette said. 'What does that involve?'

'Using and applying archaeological techniques to forensic investigations. I used to work closely with the police department in all kinds of situations: homicides, identification at mass fatalities, cold cases... Now I mainly lecture, although I do get dragged back on occasion.'

'Sounds more gruesome than my job as a police officer,' Juliette noted.

'Gruesome but rewarding,' Jack answered, before facing Morton. 'You know what got me started?'

Morton shook his head.

'The fire. There were some pretty suspicious circumstances going on there and I just couldn't let it go.'

'I thought it was accidental—caused by the Christmas tree lights?' Morton countered.

'Yeah—that was the official verdict. Afterwards, I became more and more convinced that my dad had started it deliberately. From out in San Francisco I made some discreet enquiries. I contacted the Chief Medical Examiner, who issued me my dad's autopsy report, which obviously didn't make a great deal of sense to me, so I took it along to the university and spoke to one of the professors there and I ended up joining his course. The fire became my pet project throughout the degree.'

'And did you find evidence that it was deliberate?'

Jack nodded. 'Yeah, I did.'

'But why?' Juliette asked.

'Because my dad was still married to his first wife and she was threatening to expose him—'

'What? But I found records for the divorce,' Morton interjected.

'She—his first wife, Audrey, refused it. He bigamously married my mom.'

'And so he started the fire deliberately and killed himself?' Morton questioned.

'No,' Jack replied. 'The autopsy notes showed evidence that his neck had been broken *before* the fire. The Chief Medical Examiner had dismissed it since most of his bones were broken by the house falling on top of him.'

'You're saying he hanged himself?' Morton asked.

'That's right,' Jack confirmed. 'The more time has passed, the more cases I've worked on, the more certain I am about it. It's really hard for me because in the months leading up to the fire, we weren't on good terms and I blamed him for a lot of things that weren't actually his fault.'

'So, if he'd killed himself, then who started the fire?' Juliette chipped in.

'Your mum,' Morton answered for him.

Jack nodded. 'I think my dad killed himself because of what I was finding out about his past. I think he thought it was a way to draw a line in the sand and finally put a stop to it all. My mom found his body in the basement, then she started the fire to cover up his suicide.'

'Wow...' Morton said.

'Yeah,' Jack agreed. 'And that's not all. It got me thinking about my dad's first wife. She died in 1954, along with her daughter, Florence and her lover—a guy called Dwight. They were also killed in a fire.'

'What?' Morton stammered, struggling to take in this latest information, and fearing where his line of thinking was taking him.

'It took a while after I finished college and built up some contacts in the police and fire departments and with local coroners, but I was able to get hold of the original reports into the fire. The verdict was inconclusive but one theory was that it started with an electrical heater in the basement. It was the middle of the night and the three bodies were discovered in their beds.'

'Oh my God,' Juliette mumbled. 'You think that was her, too?'

'Well, let me tell you this: the fire happened a week after my mom and dad were discovered by a private investigator that Audrey had hired to bring him to court to face charges of bigamy.'

'You're saying your mum started that fire, knowing that it would kill the three of them, including a child?' Morton said.

Jack nodded solemnly.

'Could it not just be a coincidence?' Juliette ventured.

'I don't believe in coincidences,' Jack replied.

'Neither does he,' Juliette said with a nod towards Morton.

'I didn't want to just jump to that conclusion, I really didn't. My own mom starting a fire that could have killed us all was one thing, but this was something completely different. So, I did more research. According to their neighbour at the time my mom went into a private hospital in Boston for two weeks suffering from bleeding in the early stages of her pregnancy with Alice. My dad drove her to the hospital for complete bed rest, picking her up again two weeks later.'

'Giving her just the right amount of time to cross the country…' Morton said.

'Exactly the right amount of time, when you plot possible bus and train routes that she would have taken,' Jack said. 'I also found some witnesses and possible sightings along the route, but still it was circumstantial. Then I made enquiries at the hospital in Boston and they had no record of her ever having stayed there. In fact, nobody at all was admitted during that two-week period.'

'Wow…' Morton breathed.

'Sorry,' Jack said. 'I wasn't planning on blurting it out like that. In fact, I wasn't planning on telling you right away.'

'I take it you've kept all this to yourself?' Juliette asked. 'I mean, from the police.'

'Just Alice, Jan, Laura, George and I know the truth—and now you two. I wrestled with it for a long time, I really did. I still don't know if I did the right thing. Once I had gathered enough evidence, I flew over to Boston and drove up to see my mom—the first time since I'd left in seventy-six. I stood on her doorstep and told her everything I knew. She slammed the door in my face and I walked away.'

'What an evil woman,' Juliette said. 'And ill.'

'It pains me to say it, but yes, she was,' Jack agreed. 'Alice and I talked it over—about getting the police involved—but by this time her dementia was kicking in and we just couldn't see what was to gain by putting everyone through an investigation.'

'I understand that,' Morton said.

There was a pause whilst the three of them took stock of the new revelations.

'Sorry,' Jack apologised, 'that was pretty intense for our first meeting. I promise there's nothing else bad like that.'

Morton laughed. It was funny to hear the depth of research that his father had undertaken in order to discover the truth; it was exactly what he would have done in his position.

'I hate to say this,' Juliette began, 'but we've got a plane to catch.'

'So, where do we go from here?' Jack asked. 'I mean, I know you're flying to New York then back home, but after that? I'm assuming after all that hard work that you'd like to keep in touch? Unless I've scared you off with my stories, that is.'

'Yes—yes, absolutely I'd like to stay in touch.' Morton said, lamenting that the words sounded so inadequate, like he was saying goodbye to someone whom he had just met on holiday. Now that he had found him, he wanted so much more from his relationship with his father. 'Skype? Or maybe meet up soon?'

Jack smiled. 'Yeah, I would love that. I'll get arranging a vacation to England, then. How does that sound?'

'Fantastic,' Morton replied. 'You can stay with us—we live in Rye.'

Jack's eyes lit up. 'Ah, yes, I remember quaint little Rye. Mermaid Street—is that there?'

'That's where we live,' Juliette said. 'Not a single straight wall or horizontal floor. Oh, and we have two front doors. Obviously.'

'Sounds like my kind of place,' Jack responded enthusiastically. 'And you're welcome out in Canada with us—anytime. It'll be great to have you stay with us—meet Laura and George.'

'That would be amazing,' Morton said.

'Hey—we need to exchange numbers otherwise it'll be another forty years' trying to find each other.'

Morton laughed and fished in his bag. With a trembling hand, he pulled out a business card, adding to the back every additional contact detail not already on it. Jack reciprocated and then, reluctantly Morton stood, signalling the end of one of the most momentous occasions in his entire life. At that moment, he knew that those thirty minutes with his father, whatever the future brought them, would stay with him for his whole life.

Jack stood and hugged Juliette, then turned back to Morton. 'Come here, son.' He said it with a hint of joviality, but the words were everything that Morton had ever wanted to hear.

Morton smiled and embraced his father. 'Goodbye.'

'You know, you could always join us for a few days in New York,' Juliette suggested. 'If you're free.'

Jack looked uncertain. 'On your honeymoon?'

Juliette looked at Morton. 'Fine by me—obviously.'

Morton nodded. 'That would be amazing if you could get a flight down?'

'I'll tell you what I'll do,' Jack said. 'I'm going to get a rental car and go up and see my sister for a couple of days, give you guys some time alone, then I'll drive down to see you in the city—how's that?'

'Perfect,' Morton said.

'I'll be touch, then,' Jack said. 'Now go and catch your flight.'

'Bye.'

The queue at check-in had dissolved and they went straight through, pausing as they disappeared through security to give Jack one last wave as he watched them leave.

Morton emitted a long, meaningful sigh as they collected their hand luggage from the security conveyer belt, tears returning to his eyes again, as he took in the magnitude of the situation. 'Well...that was unexpected—my God.'

Juliette kissed him on the lips. 'See, I knew you'd find him in the end. Although, technically, it was actually *me* who found him, but I'll let that one pass.'

Morton laughed and reached for her hand. 'Come on, we've got a few minutes—let's go and grab a glass of champagne.'

Juliette turned her nose up. 'Naaah—just a lemonade will do.'

'Oh come off it—I've just met my dad—I want to *celebrate*.'

Juliette pulled Morton to a stop and stood in front of him. 'We can—but with lemonade.'

'I don't understand. Why are you grinning like that?'

'Well...we've got something else to celebrate: I'm pregnant.'

'What?'

'I'm pregnant.'

'Lemonade all round!' Morton shouted, lifting Juliette off the ground and kissing her on the lips.

Acknowledgments

Much of the research for this book came during a two-week trip to Massachusetts in October 2016. During that time, I visited various locations, libraries and repositories, where I received considerable help and advice. Therefore, my thanks must go to the following: the staff of the genealogy section of Boston Public Library; the staff of vital records in Boston City Hall; Karen Horn at Sturgis Library; Leslie Steers at Barnstable Town Hall; and David Allen Lambert and Fr David Frederici for their knowledge of Cape Cod. All of the records that Morton uses in his research are real, but with fictitious content.

Whilst undertaking my research, I had the pleasure of meeting with the Writing Family History Special Interest Group of the Cape Cod Genealogical Society. The group were extremely helpful in answering my queries and questions, so thank you to the following, too: David Martin, Joan Frederici, Alice Plouchard Stelzer, Andrea Forbes, Madeline McHugh, and Priscilla Ryan.

My thanks also go to Gail Ann Pippin for her Boston dinner suggestion—Legal Seafood—a good choice!

As always, I am very grateful to Patrick Dengate for turning my vague ideas into a much better book cover than I could have imagined.

Thanks to my early readers, Pauline Daniels, Patrick Dengate and Joan Frederici for all their suggestions and amendments, and thanks to my proof-reader, Julia Gibbs.

Lastly, for too many things to possibly list, my heartfelt thanks go to Robert Bristow.

Further information:

Website: www.nathandylangoodwin.com
Twitter: @nathangoodwin76
Facebook: www.facebook.com/nathandylangoodwin
Pinterest: www.pinterest.com/dylan0470/
Blog: theforensicgenealogist.blogspot.co.uk

Praise for *Hiding the Past*
(The Forensic Genealogist #1)

'Flicking between the present and stories and extracts from the past, the pace never lets up in an excellent addition to this unique genre of literature' *Your Family Tree*

'At times amusing and shocking, this is a fast-moving modern crime mystery with genealogical twists. The blend of well fleshed-out characters, complete with flaws and foibles, will keep you guessing until the end' *Family Tree*

'Once I started reading *Hiding the Past* I had great difficulty putting it down - not only did I want to know what happened next, I actually cared' *Lost Cousins*

'This is a must read for all genealogy buffs and anyone who loves a good mystery with a jaw dropping ending!' *Baytown Genealogy Society*

'This is a good read and will appeal to anyone interested in family history. I can thoroughly recommend it' *Cheshire Ancestor*

'*Hiding the Past* is a suspenseful, fast-paced mystery novel, in which the hero is drawn into an intrigue that spans from World War II to the present, with twists and turns along the way. The writing is smooth and the story keeps moving along so that I found it difficult to put down' *The Archivist*

Praise for *The Lost Ancestor*
(The Forensic Genealogist #2)

'If you enjoy a novel with a keen eye for historical detail, solid writing, believable settings and a sturdy protagonist, *The Lost Ancestor* is a safe bet. Here British author Nathan Dylan Goodwin spins a riveting genealogical crime mystery with a pulsing, realistic storyline' *Your Family Tree*

'Finely paced and full of realistic genealogical terms and tricks, this is an enjoyable whodunit with engaging research twists that keep you guessing until the end. If you enjoy genealogical fiction and Ruth Rendell mysteries, you'll find this a pleasing page-turner' *Family Tree*

'...an extremely well-constructed plot, with plenty of intrigue and genealogical detail - but all the loose ends are neatly tied up by the end... *The Lost Ancestor* is highly recommended' *Lost Cousins*

'It's an excellent pick for holidays, weekend relaxing, or curling up indoors or outdoors, whatever the weather permits in your corner of the world' *Lisa Louise Cooke*

'*The Lost Ancestor* is fast-paced, not plodding, and does well building mystery... The author's depictions of scenes and places are vivid; the characters are interesting and intriguing. In toggling back and forth from past to present, Goodwin shows how the deeds of long-dead ancestors are haunting their descendants' *GenealogyMagazine.com*

'It's entertaining, and passes the time nicely while setting the chores aside... just the right kind of light reading we need during this time of holiday busyness' *Eastman's Online Genealogy*

Praise for *The America Ground*
(The Forensic Genealogist #3)

'As in the earlier novels, each chapter slips smoothly from past to present, revealing murderous events as the likeable Morton uncovers evidence in the present, while trying to solve the mystery of his own paternity. Packed once more with glorious detail of records familiar to family historians, *The America Ground* is a delightfully pacey read' *Family Tree*

'Like most genealogical mysteries this book has several threads, cleverly woven together by the author - and there are plenty of surprises for the reader as the story approaches its conclusion. A jolly good read!' *Lost Cousins*

'Goodwin's stories have been good reads, engaging the interest of the genealogist with references to records…Readers will welcome this new book as a welcome distraction from the intensity of research to reading about someone else's work, with murder thrown in' *Eastman's Online Genealogy Newsletter*

'Great reading - a real page-turner! Good solid genealogy research – highly recommended' *Genealogy Happy Hour*

'It's just a terrific book! It's great stuff, I've read it, and you're going to enjoy it' *Extreme Genes*

'The writing is pin-sharp and there is plenty of suspense in an excellent novel which makes me want to return to the first books in the series' *The Norfolk Ancestor*

'This is a good crime novel with links to family history and in it you have the best of both worlds…the twisting story will keep you guessing to the last page' *The Wakefield Kinsman*

Praise for *The Spyglass File*
(The Forensic Genealogist #4)

'If you like a good mystery, and the detective work of genealogy, this is another mystery novel from Nathan which will have you whizzing through the pages with time slipping by unnoticed'
Your Family History

'The first page was so overwhelming that I had to stop for breath...Well, the rest of the book certainly lived up to that impressive start, with twists and turns that kept me guessing right to the end... As the story neared its conclusion I found myself conflicted, for much as I wanted to know how Morton's assignment panned out, I was enjoying it so much that I really didn't want this book to end!'
Lost Cousins

'Author Nathan Dylan Goodwin has given students of the Second World War, and avid family historians another great genealogical read'
Eastman's Online Genealogy Newsletter

'Nathan Dylan Goodwin's latest Morton Farrier genealogical mystery deserves its five-star reviews on Amazon. A gripping story that will have you sneaking away to read just one more chapter!'
Historian

'Like his previous books, also set in England, this one keeps you intrigued right up to the very end... His style of weaving the past and present together is outstanding'
Bay Area Genealogical Society

'A really good read and a mystery which holds you to the end'
The Wakefield Kidsman

Printed in Great Britain
by Amazon